ARISE AND THRESH

By Anderson E. McClure

A person's mental illness can only be measured by how well adapted they are to a profoundly abnormal society.

-Aldous Huxley

This work is dedicated to all the White men and women around the world who still want to preserve the purity of their race

Table of Contents

ARISE AND THRESH

Chapter 1

Leaving

Life in my rural Kentucky home provided me with a wonderful childhood. Although my father passed away relatively young, I had other men who influenced my life. My grandfather, Ephraim, had always been my best friend. I know the loss of his own son must have been hard for him, but he put a lot of time and effort into my raising when he could have done other things. I grew up going to public school before it became completely over-run by the communists. I was however able to pick up on some of the anti-white narrative being peddled, even back then, but those thoughts get in the way of teenage happiness. Tiffany and I were high school sweethearts, and it was a normal, healthy, teenage relationship. I played sports while she cheered, and we ran cross-country together. Most people said we were a beautiful couple, and we married shortly after high school. For the most part, I lived a normal life; blissfully ignorant of the political world which didn't seem important. It wasn't until my early twenties that I began to realize the decay and

1

moral decline that lay beneath it all. By the time Tiffany and I became serious, our town had already experienced large numbers of illegal farm workers who over ran our grocery and department stores. It was what I considered a minor nuisance at the time because I had no concept of the geopolitical storm that was being manufactured against White people all over the world, let alone in my own hometown. Throughout the following years, we endured riots, looting and burning of our cities. The monuments to our fallen heroes had been desecrated along with their graves. Gay pride parades followed along with drag queens demonstrating in our public schools and local libraries. Our daughter Lia suffered by way of confusion from the degenerate demonstrations that were allowed to proceed without parental consent. I fought tooth and nail to convince Tiffany and anyone who would listen not to succumb to the fear of the fake viruses that the mainstream media would peddle on a daily basis. Every few months society was told they needed a different vaccine and lots of people I knew and had even admired, fell for the propaganda. I became so outspoken that Tiffany began to be afraid. She was not on board with the level of radicalization that I had reached. I sort of understood. She wanted a normal life, free from too much responsibility when it came to the world outside her own. It was denial that kept her from moving forward with me. I was interested in fighting to secure a future for our daughter, even if it meant being doxed at work or sacrificing my reputation and allowing the world to call me racist or White supremist or any other names that Whites get labeled in order to keep them from rising above the shame that they have been taught to have about themselves by those that hate them. There had been some 'White flight' from our area into other areas of larger White populations which also allowed homes to be bought up by outsiders and city people running from their collapsing suburban dreams. 'White flight' is a phenomenon that occurs when multiculturalism is forced

2

on Whites. White people always flock to be among other Whites because where they are found, societies are predominantly peaceful. In stark contrast, the other races run from the violent, even cannibalistic societies in some cases, and run into White nations to pilfer, beg, murder, and rape their way into an otherwise peaceful society. The majority of the people in any given rural conservative Kentucky town, continued down the path of wasting all their effort by always voting for a new liar, which I saw as absolutely futile. None of the issues I wanted to address were ever even talked about in debates, or anywhere else for that matter. It was as if the White colonial stock that built America didn't exist. Every candidate ran on the promise to help this or that minority in order to secure the vote, because Whites were losing their dominance and control of their own country. The only thing that they seemed to agree on was that America had to stand beside that middle eastern 'ally' who did absolutely nothing to deserve the title. The dual citizenship held by all of our representatives and the lobbying babysitters made it pretty easy for someone of average intelligence to put two and two together; but the brainwashing was so complete that few seemed able to break free from it. Every piece of legislation which passed, had language detrimental to the success of White people. The more I felt ostracized by my own government, the more vocal I became. I took a lot of heat from family members during holidays as they all expected me to jump on board with their new political savior even though I gave them facts about useless policies that kept us on a path of decline. They were never able to digest the facts or, that legal third-world scum was the same as illegal third-world scum. The people of these cultures cannot maintain the world Whites built for themselves, and to sate that fact in public was seen only as racist. A political solution had become laughable, but it entertained millions into watching and believing that there were nonviolent answers to our oppression. They simply could not grasp that the present system

3

was incapable of stopping the growth of Marxism, and certainly not capable of restoring what had already been given away. This was the scenario playing out in real time as I begin this story of how my radicalization accelerated beyond the point of no return.

Tiffany and I had been divorced for almost 18 months. My simple lifestyle unfortunately did not measure up to the ideal dream life that she had imagined for herself as we entered our thirties. Although she was more than happy to meet me for the purpose of satisfying our physical needs on more than one occasion during the court proceedings, it wasn't enough to keep her from the arms of a local practicing doctor. Dr. Vane was a womanizing creep who Tiffany had seen for her recurring headaches, and, evidently, he gave her more than a prescription. No doubt he was smitten by her charm and sexuality, and he had the funds to keep her happy. I see her every other weekend when I get our daughter and she isn't exactly flirtatious, but she loves to point out the negative aspects of my very rural life, in an 'opposites attract' sort of way. I believe she did this for two reasons. On one hand, she did miss me and was probably not as happy as she thought she would be, and on the other hand, she wanted to make me feel as though she had left me for good reason to alleviate her guilt. I had discovered her new beau's extra source of income through some detective means and my hatred for him grew exponentially. He had become president of an NGO that was bringing migrants into our community by the thousands. I had no idea if Tiffany was aware of it, or if she understood the implications it would have for our home and our daughter.

Our house was sold but I didn't want to live there anyway, and she allowed me to keep my Granddad's farm, which I inherited shortly before our daughter was born. I built a small, tiny home on a rather large tract of wooded land and then allowed a few trees to be logged, which in turn gave me some financial cushion and plenty of work to be done. I had been hauling wood to people during the fall and winter to buy a few things, and in the summer I worked seasonal work at the golf course, helping out with mowing and building maintenance. It was the kind of life that was simple, until Tiffany made life difficult. In order to deal with the stresses of a disappearing White civilization and the ruin of society as a whole, I had basically retreated to my cabin in the woods. Prior to our divorce, I had begun to notice some patterns in politics and media which began to shape my worldview in ways which would get me labeled a "racist." Things had gotten so bad with the gay agenda at the local library and other stores in town, that I publicly made my alt-right position clear to anyone who would listen.

I did some individual activism because no one seemed able to rise above their own self-censorship. Talking to people about the dangers that were already happening before their eyes and having them stare blank faced as if they had no clue what was happening around them, was disheartening.

I created stickers to place at the gas pumps that read: "Deport Sand Niggers Now!" I would pick up golf balls during my summer job and write, "I love being White", and then toss them out for others to find. I even hung a banner from an overpass in the dark of night that read: "Death to ZOG". This was my most daring act, and it brought me a huge rush to be able to do something, or anything instead of nothing, while my home was invaded and destroyed. I had been a sports fan and watched religiously as a young man and would identify with teams and the negro athletes who dominated American sports. The only white people I saw during many sporting events were the beautiful, white cheerleaders as they cheered for their negro idols with dreadlocks and diseases. I began to see that my television was basically slapping my race down with nearly every movie, sitcom, and commercial. And heroic White men were nowhere to be found. If I was to become extinct or homeless in the land my fathers gave me, it was not going to be my fault. Nor could I look myself in the mirror and know, that while I watched niggers bounce balls and flex after slamming it through a hoop, my daughter's future was being stolen from under my nose. I had become very bitter and lonely.

One Sunday afternoon, after meeting Tiffany at the school parking lot to give our daughter back for two weeks, she gave me an inclination that something wasn't going well for her at home. Her pouty expression came across as though she wanted me to ask her if something was wrong, but I wasn't in the mood for her manipulative games. I just gave her my usual coldness, which she deserved, but she gave me a considerable amount of eye contact which I hadn't seen from her in years. Her full lips and designer clothes along with her straight, platinum blonde hair made her very attractive to any man; but, as I saw her that day, I realized she might have thought herself to be out of my league. I was a little rough around the edges, maybe too rough for Tiffany. I was unrepentant in my role as an alpha male, but Tiffany needed someone to baby her and I needed her to grow up. As she approached her car door, her gaze lingered for what seemed like an eternity before she let it drop, and then she looked again in my direction before driving away. I waved at our daughter in the backseat until they were out of sight and then climbed back in my truck. I sat there silently for a few moments. I was fighting emotions. Tiffany was my first love, she was the mother of my child, and she was also smoking hot, but she had not only broken my heart, but she also shattered it. I wanted so badly to hate her, but I couldn't. I sat there in my truck and fantasized about having her in my little cabin. I undressed her slowly in my mind like I had done so many times before. I knew how she felt under my hands, and I wanted to feel her again. I wanted to hear her moans

6

again as I pleasured her. Then my phone interrupted my thoughts. It was an unknown number with a text that read:

"I saw your ad for firewood at the hardware store. Do you still have some for sale?"

I replied, "yes", got the address, (which sounded vaguely familiar), and agreed to bring the wood the following morning. I took a deep breath and pulled away from the parking lot toward my rural retreat somewhat disillusioned and defeated. I was beginning to think I might have to face the perils of a collapsing world alone.

I got back to the cabin after dark, but I went ahead and loaded the wood so that I would be ready to deliver it in the morning. Cold showers are invigorating. I hadn't been able to purchase a water heater due to the new laws requiring a plumber's license to purchase one. This was just one in a long line of stupid things where governments think they need to intervene. I rekindled the fire in my stove and all I could think about was rekindling a fire with Tiffany. I started to get angry with myself and decided that this was all her fault. She didn't deserve any sympathy for anything that she might be going through now, because she brought it on herself. I lay on my mattress and surveyed the contents of my home. My rifle by my bed, the picture of Lia and I fishing, the painting of Christ walking on water. I glanced at the picture of Davis under the battle flag and Adolf under the NSDAP flag I had acquired, and then at the picture of my granddad, who brought about my very existence on the land where I now live. With that thought in mind, I went to bed.

As I pulled up to the address the next morning to deliver the firewood, I recognized the car in the driveway. I was pretty sure it belonged to Jessica, a second cousin of Tiffany's. She was about five or six years younger than Tiffany and was certainly on par as her equal in every physical aspect. Her choice in men happened to be terrible however, and last year he was finally locked up for battery and assault. Apparently, she had been injured somehow in an argument that led to his arrest, which led to more charges and eventually felony time. I remember seeing her at a few of the family reunions and thinking about how she could have done so much better for herself than she did. We never spoke on those occasions, nor were we ever introduced, but our eyes had met, and I could tell that she was more than just aware of my existence. Truth be told, I had fantasized about her several times, purely out of lust for her body, and the eyes that she looked at me with, but never considered giving her much more than a second thought. I had always been happy in my marriage and Tiffany never had anything good to say about her. I attributed it to the fact that she was possibly jealous of her looks. Jessica was slightly taller, which gave her a thinner appearance. I couldn't say for certain, but it is possible that she had implants because she was very firm and round in her chest. Tiffany did not get her breastwork done until she was able to get them paid for by her new man. They both were stunningly beautiful in my opinion and had I not been the same age as Tiffany when we met, I would have been extremely attracted to Jessica. Somewhere in their family was a breakdown of class structure. Tiffany's parents were financially secure enough to give her all she ever needed growing up. Jessica's situation was quite different. Her dad was a biker. He was in and out of her life during her formative years and had not been the most involved father or husband. She had an older brother who was killed in a motorcycle accident when he was eighteen and it lead to a domestic dispute between her mom and derelict father, who she blamed. Jessica's mom, Doris, was beaten harshly before she shot him with a .22 pistol. She only winged him but it was enough to stop him. He fled and never went to the hospital, nor was he apprehended.

8

Jessica married a man who was as low down as her dad was.

The outside of the house was a disaster. It was obvious that there wasn't a man around and although the house had been nice at one time, it was going to need attention soon. As I came up the steps, I heard the door open and sure enough, she nearly gasped at the sight of me.

"I know you!" she said as she covered her mouth with her hand. She took her hand away from her face and smiled, then motioned for me to come inside the door. I immediately felt hot, like I was about to melt. She was extremely sexy. Blonde hair put up in the back, barefoot in her pajama bottoms and a pullover over her bra, which was yellow and showing. One thing country girls can find without trouble is a tanning bed. Jessica's skin looked like she had just gotten back from the Caribbean and the fact that I could smell a hint of coconut lotion sent my heart into a race. I hadn't been alone with or around a woman for a year and a half and my sexual tension was peaking so that I could barely think. I honestly had no intention of acting on any of the thoughts that were going through my head, but they were coming so fast and strong that I could hardly reply when she asked, "How have you been since the divorce?"

"Uh...ok, I guess...I mean, I'm getting by. How about you...since your...situation happened?"

She chuckled a bit and said, "I don't miss that bastard...he tried to kill me."

She handed me a cup of cider and then looked at me with those eyes that I remembered, and I was sure that she remembered my eyes as well. With her smile gone she said, "I never understood what the fuck Tiffany was thinking, leaving you..."

9

I was always shocked when elegant looking women used foul language and somewhat turned on. I was learning quickly that I was out of my comfort zone. Her eyes traveled the length of me. Years of physical work and outdoor living had chiseled my physique and given me a healthy complexion. I was straight and broad shouldered and probably looked like a lumberjack with my beard and toboggin.

"Lots of talk going around whether you're single still. I mean a girl would be crazy not to want to be with you."

Her eyes held me. She began to fiddle with the string on her pajama bottoms as she looked down and then back at me. Then she turned quickly as if to clear her mind and asked about our daughter. As she stepped into the kitchen, I had no control over watching her as she walked.

"She seems to be managing ok," I said robotically. She quickly returned and inquisitively asked, "Do you see Tiffany much?"

I was somewhat shocked about being interrogated by this beautiful young woman, but she was so easy to talk to. There was an obvious elephant in the room and we both knew it. How had fate conveniently decided that two freshly single attractive people would be alone in a room together, mulling over our relationship status?

"I don't" I said matter-of-factly. "And I try not to think about her," I lied. Her body language was clearly conveying that she would gladly remove all thoughts of Tiffany from my brain. She moved a few steps closer and asked in a low voice, "Are you seeing...anyone?" She could see that I was suffering. God she was hot. I tried to play it off.

"So…uh, where…uh..." I swallowed hard, "where do you want me to put the… (deep breath) …wood?"

By now I could see her breathing had changed as well. She was not quick to answer. She hesitated as she ran her tongue over her lips. She reached up to take the banana clip from her hair and I could see her bottoms were barely clinging to her hips. Her navel was pierced with a stud. Her hair came down all messy to her shoulders as she moved close to me and reached for me.

"You can put it anywhere you like."

After that, I don't remember putting my drink down and I don't remember how my clothes were removed. I was completely intoxicated with this girl. It was a frantic, primal instinct kind of sex from that point forward. She wanted me as badly as I wanted her. I remember her gray bottoms dropping to the floor as we were kissing passionately. I gripped both her ass cheeks and spread them and squeezed them as she pressed herself into me. I picked her up off the floor as she wrapped her long tanned legs around me and suspended herself as I cradled her by her ass. With a couple of fingers, I felt of her. She was soaking her tiny yellow bikini bottom through with her natural lubricant. My God, had she been planning this? I thought. She gasped with anticipation as I ran my finger back and forth and then gently penetrating ever so slightly. I took a few steps with her in my arms and rested her on a bar in the kitchen entrance never relinquishing the tongue hold we had on each other. Once I was free, I paused momentarily for her to change her mind, maybe, or get absolute approval, possibly...but regardless, it was the last chance at coherent thought for either of us. I pulled away from her lips and looked into her eyes. I had rarely seen desire like this. It was impulsive, to say the least, but she never slowed down. She went straight for me, and I heard her muffle the words, "oh gawd" just as she took me in her mouth. She stood up after a few moments, took my hand, and led me to the couch. She turned her back to me as she bent over, and her yearning was an audible whining and whimpering like a dog in heat. Her body was flawless. She did have a jagged scar on her left shoulder which was no real surprise considering the life I knew she had been exposed to. I never questioned or hesitated. I let all my cares go. I knew in my subconscious that what we were doing was irresponsible but the high overtook me.

I had to pull out rather quickly to avoid leaving her in the dust. It had been too long for me. She turned to me with a look of desperation and impatience. She led me to her unmade bed and by that time I was ready to go again. I caressed every inch of her before we continued. She raised her legs to take me deeper and her moans mixed with her exclamations of the word "fuck" nearly caused me to lose it. I pulled out again and she sat up to meet me and shoved me onto my back. She climbed onto me and worked herself back and forth. I hit a spot in her that hadn't been hit in a while because she lost control faster than I expected. She convulsed and trembled uncontrollably but seemed unashamed to allow me to see her in such a vulnerable state. Her firm breasts bounced as she did. She must have been at least confident enough in her appearance to let me see her this way...and it was glorious. We rolled over again, and I gave her myself to the fullest. I couldn't slow down at the end if I had tried and she was begging me,

"Please don't stop Zach...oh please don't stop, please give me all of it…"

So, I let go with long deep, calculated thrusts that caused her to swear over and over. My mind and body were exploding with pleasure to the point that I couldn't comprehend what was happening. I felt my load leaving in torrents as it entered into the womb of my ex-wife's younger cousin...and she seemed to want it without reserve. When it was over, we were both exasperated. Her breasts were heaving with accelerated breathing, and I was convinced that they were natural...her nipples so hard and erect with goosebumps of tiny, microscopic blonde hairs standing on end. I kissed her gently for several moments while I remained inside her.

She felt so amazing; I had no words. We eventually settled into a tangled leg position with her head on my chest and my arm around her. I caressed her hair gently. She slowly propped herself up to get a closer look at the Eagle and swastika tattoo on my right upper chest. She traced the lines with her finger and then looked intently into my face. She remained silent and lay her head back on my chest. If she had been born in a different place other than rural Kentucky, she could have been a model. I lay there with the knowledge that I had just completely thrown caution to the wind. I really didn't know this girl and I wasn't truly over the feelings I had for Tiffany, but I sincerely needed to feel love again. After about an hour she gently initiated a slow kiss, then got up without saying a word. After I got my clothes on and we cleaned up, I told her I would unload my truck in the shed. She demanded on paying after I told her it wasn't necessary. I think she didn't want me thinking she was trying to get firewood in exchange for sex. I knew better anyway. A woman who initiates that kind of sex was in need of something more than firewood. As I was leaving, it quickly occurred to me that there was no reason for talking. The chemistry between us was running very deep, almost like I had known her all my life. I seemed to understand her need and she seemed to understand mine. Talking about it might ruin the magic of it all.

Once I was on my way, it took me a few moments to comprehend what had just happened. I was somewhat in shock and somewhat excited and, along with that, I was feeling out of control.

13

I had without doubt enjoyed the sex and admired the beauty of this woman, but what would transpire now. The psychological impact of sexual behavior rarely comes without a price. I knew little to nothing about Jessica other than the negative highlights that Tiffany painted for me. I didn't even know if she was legally separated from her abusive husband. Also, I wondered how she seemed so ready for me. Women like to take time to prepare for sex and Jessica was more than fully prepared when I arrived. It just seemed odd. I didn't linger on those particulars because ultimately, I didn't care. I wasn't beholden to Tiffany anymore and she had obviously moved on. If I wanted to pursue a new relationship, I was free to do so. I also wondered what she really thought of my tattoo. It had caught her eye and like most people, (I was certain she was no different), she had likely never considered any version of history other than the Jew version. I had to admit that my transformation into a ZOG-hating neo nazi, (that's what the ADL calls me), probably affected Tiffany more than I wanted to admit. I was too outspoken and too willing to sacrifice my reputation by being labeled a racist that I think she began distancing herself from me emotionally. She couldn't argue with the things I would say but I think it scared her, or maybe the indoctrination was too much for her. I wondered if my need for acceptance and the need to be loved was what allowed Jessica to take full control of my thoughts or was I genuinely feeling compassion for her. Was this purely lust? No, I thought. I was already missing her; I wanted to bring her home with me. Was I falling in love with her? I may have already fallen. Before I pulled into my drive, I felt my phone buzz in my pocket. I stopped the truck and shut it off. It was a message from the unknown number that I now know is Jessica. It simply read, "thank you." I replied, "the pleasure was all mine."

I sat high in my deer stand until nearly dark, which was about

4:30 PM in early January. My grandfather taught me young how to hunt and the simple joys of being in nature. I killed my first deer at a young age and because rifle hunting had become too easy for me, I decided to hunt in the early fall and early winter with my bow and leave modern gun season to the wannabe hunters from the suburban areas. So many farmers around me had leased their farms out to companies who basically pimped out our culture and sold the meat out from under our local people. I sat for many hours in the woods thinking and brewing over the years how I could possibly make a difference or change the course society was taking. I felt hopeless and angry most of the time. I took a shot at a young deer with my bow and heard it fall just out of sight behind a fallen oak tree where briars had taken over a fencerow. I had climbed out of my stand and was about to take my first step in the direction of my kill when I heard gravel popping near my house almost three-hundred yards away. I had been unable to remove the events of that morning from my mind and I was guilty of wishfully thinking that Jessica had come to find me. My phone buzzed. It was Tiffany.

"Are you home?"

"I'm in the woods, be there in a minute."

This was a strange occurrence. Tiffany rarely came alone to see me. As I approached her, she was standing beside her car with her arms folded and shivering. She looked as though she had been crying. (I knew that look all too well). She had cut her hair, still sexy and well dressed.

"What's going on?"

"Zach, I shouldn't be here but I gotta tell you something..."

With all that had happened in the last 24 hours, the sky was the limit with what she was about to say, and I was a bit nervous actually.

"There's been a government proposal for a land development. I saw the emails."

"Whoa...slow down." I did my best to calm her so that she could properly speak. She was shivering and emotional.

"It's for housing! To bring in more of these goddamned sand niggers."

My heart nearly leapt for joy at the sound of her saying something so profound and indignant. Maybe there was hope for her yet.

"You were right Zach! And they want your land!" There was a pause as I let the brevity of her statement soak in.

"What? How? Why?"

"I don't know the details; all I know is that I saw the plat and the design. It had property owners' names listed. You know these things can't be stopped. I've overheard conversations."

"Ok, ok." I tried again to calm her as she bowed her pretty head. When she looked back up at me, tears had filled the corners of her eyes.

"I'm Sorry Zach," she said in a cracked voice. She moved quickly to her car, wiping tears and sniffling the whole way. I stood there motionless until her taillights disappeared into the night. I couldn't figure out if she meant she was sorry that the government wanted my land, or if she was sorry she had filed for our divorce. Maybe she meant both. Coyotes howled.

I knew I had no time to waste. I brushed it all to the back of my mind as best I could for the moment and grabbed a light to go retrieve the deer. I had left my bow in the woods, so I grabbed my AR from the truck in order to deal with those predators...but by the time I got there, very little of my deer was left. I stood there in the middle of the woods in disbelief. I was standing there just taking the waves as they hit me, my emotions everywhere, trying to hold onto sanity. The beautiful morning with Jessica seemed a distant memory now amidst the tidal wave of news Tiffany had just delivered. I couldn't fret over the lost deer; I needed to get back to the cabin to sort through some thoughts and do a little research. Just as I neared the cabin, headlights blasted me and then big fog lights on a Kentucky Fish & Wildlife truck. Good lord what else can go wrong I thought. I was standing there with a rifle, in my hunting clothes, out of rifle season, and chances were that the officer was that little prick Delwin who jacks off to his badge every night. He's so power and ego driven that the academy should have never graduated a jerk like him.

"Looks like you have some explaining to do Wayne" then he laughed cockily. We've known each other since middle school, and he knows I don't go by my middle name.

"What do you want asshole?" I called him by the name he should have been given at birth. He laughed again, not because he thought I was funny but because he knew I was going to meet him with every ounce of resistance I could muster without forcing him to call for back up.

"Well, I came to give you a little heads up, old friend," he said sarcastically. "Big money's coming to this town. Rumor is you're going to get to be a part of it."

"I don't want to be a part of it" I said quickly. Delwin looked like a confused puppy dog with his head cocked to the side.

"What do you mean, you don't even know what...." he paused, and wheels began to turn in his head, and I felt I may have made a terrible mistake. I'm not sure what his connections to this money were but it was likely in the same connections or circles that Tiffany was in, and the puzzle was coming together for both of us in real time. I wasn't supposed to know, and the only way I could have known is if someone close to Delwin's connections told me, and I could tell he knew. He was a dick for sure, but he wasn't stupid. He turned in silence. "You'll be getting the fine in the mail. I'll let you keep the gun for now and we'll let the judge decide if he wants to confiscate it." What he meant was, he will go back and write up the paperwork to have a SWAT team come and confiscate my gun, or anything else they want. It had become standard operating procedure, and I had already seen it happen to other men who were possible threats to their corruption. He backed out of my drive and rolled down his window before he pulled away, "Don't let the bed bugs bite." He chuckled at his own humor as he spun gravel like a teenager driving his daddy's truck. What a piece of shit I thought. I was thinking about which deep sinkhole I would put his body in when I received another text. This time it was her.

I guess she had done a considerable amount of thinking throughout the day because she asked if we could talk. She agreed to come to my cabin as if that's what she had wanted me to propose. I insisted on picking her up. It was nearing 8pm before I got to her house. I had to do a quick internet search and take one of those lovely cold showers, I mean who knew what might transpire between her and I, right? As I drove, all I could think about was the possibility that I might have put Tiffany in more danger than she was already in and also the safety of our daughter Lia. My thoughts

18

drifted to the possible relationship with Jessica, and how I was going to have to tell her that my life was about to become a shit show. As bad as I wanted to pursue a new life with her, I couldn't ask her to become involved in what was quickly becoming a train wreck for me.

She was ready at the door when I arrived. She was dressed in a long white Victorian gown as though she were ready to turn in for the night, with the exception of the mid-cut Muck boots and the camo coat she was about to throw on. She was the epitome of a hot mess but with her Germanic look, blonde hair, and full lips, she could make a deer hide look fashionable.

"You mind if I take a bag?" She had a duffle bag beside the door, and I assumed she was really asking me if she could stay the night at my place. I would be fine if she stayed at my place permanently.

"Bring several bags if you need to." I hinted with a bit of wit. She turned her head quickly to catch my eyes as I grinned shyly. A grin spread across her face that showed me she knew I had read past her words, and she liked what I had replied. I had not seen her smile that way, and although I had unconsciously noticed already, what became apparent with her smile was the line on her face that acted as a parenthesis at the corners of her mouth. Tiffany had it as well. I had always found this attractive for some unknown reason.

"I'm ready," she said. "Let's go."

The drive back to my place was very quiet. Before we could get back to the highway, she put her hand on the console of my truck and stared at it motionlessly as if she was wondering what her hand was doing there all alone. I took the wheel with my left hand and took her hand in mine. She breathed deeply and closed her eyes.

Something or lots of things had this poor, beautiful woman in such a state of inner turmoil that I was beginning to think that she was not just attracted to me physically, but that she was finding solace in something real and true. She pulled her right foot out of her boot and put her heel on the edge of the seat. I struggled to maintain focus on the road. I was fascinated by her and was having real feelings for who she was, but I could easily sexualize every inch of her body. There was no part of her that did not turn me on. We continued to ride in silence as she seemed to be resting. It felt good to provide her with the safety and security that she obviously longed for.

We pulled into my secluded drive off the 3/4-mile-long gravel road and hiked uphill to my cabin, hand in hand. Inside she looked around as she took in her surroundings and because I knew she was of above average intelligence; she was aligning her thoughts of me with what she was seeing. I was ok with that. I was deeply smitten with Jessica but there was nothing about my belief system that I was willing to compromise for anyone. If I had been willing to do that, I would have done it to keep Tiffany. No one could come into my living space and leave without fully knowing where I stood. She saw my flags and the portraits of my heroes which I will admit looked somewhat like a shrine to the demonized villains of secular history. She sat in my recliner as I suggested, and I sat facing her in my kitchen chair. She made no comments about my humble home, and she began by saying, "I don't even have a wood stove," I could tell that she was about to confess something more, so I let her talk unabatedly. She saw that I was not going to interrupt her as she looked for the answers in my expressions, but I gave her nothing but grace.

"I found out from Margie that you were delivering wood and that you had advertised at the store...she talks about you all the time." Margie was my ex-mother-in-law, and Jessica's great aunt.

"I… uh..." she stuttered and searched for words. "Ever since I saw you at those... reunions...well...I saw the way you were...I mean kind, handsome...I saw in you everything I would never have." She waited again for my reply, but this was only the beginning of the story, so I waited patiently for her to get out what she came to tell me. "I know about the boots you bought and gave to Gerald Hawkins. I know about the free loads of wood you've been giving to old Mrs. Hobbs and Dorothy Greer…I know about how they were trying to have you arrested for the things you said in front of those faggots at the library." She nearly made me hard with the last comment. After a long pause of studying my face, she began again in a cracked voice, "What I want to tell you is…well, I have longed for a man, a real man...to…to...take me..." Tears came into her eyes. I fought tears myself but was unable to succeed. I moved toward her to gently kiss her lips as the first streams came down her cheeks. I didn't know at that moment what her life must have been like, but I was going to do whatever I could to make it better. We talked into the night. She had been raped by two men when she was fourteen which she said lowered her self-worth and ultimately led to her marriage to a total loser who she had become legally separated from yesterday. Her dad was too busy in his extra-marital affairs that he couldn't be bothered by her trouble, and she remembered him doubting her word that it had even happened. One of the boys who had done the rape was a judge's son who was in her class in High School, but he was aided by an older boy who was in my class, she said. He was really cruel to her verbally during the ordeal. He was a game warden now. She began to tire of talking about the depressing aspects of her past and then her inquisitive nature beckoned her to question me.

"So... are you a White supremacist?" The tone in her raspy voice was not as though she was put off by the fact that I might be a

21

White supremacist, but rather that I was guilty of something taboo that she might also find intriguing. It was the same tone she might have used if she had said, "So... have you been staring at my tits" ...with a half grin.

I had no idea what her perception of the term meant so I began slowly with questions for her about how she felt about the world in its present decline. I had her take out her phone and look at the early life sections of online biographies of the owners at BlackRock, all the media CEOs and presidents. We looked at the major contributors of all Antifa and BLM riots and ultimately who funded the burning of our cities and the cultural replacement of Whites. We discussed the major financial contributors of the non-Governmental Organizations who were funding the migrant crisis that our hometown was undergoing. I could tell that it was a lot at once for her to take in and she was doing a lot of staring and contemplating. She needed no convincing that our situation was dire, but I was bringing the enemy in front of her, and she could see it was difficult to deny. She stared silently for a long time at the picture of Hitler and the Nazi flag on my wall.

"I thought the Jews were persecuted...Well, we all did until you started to notice patterns and things we were told from history class that made no sense."

I broke off the subject because I could see that she was well enlightened and had confidence that she wouldn't need much guidance now. She was smart.

"This all kinda brings me to a situation that I need to talk to you about..." She heard the concern in my voice. I explained to her what was happening and explained the bigger picture. Tiffany was likely in danger, and maybe my daughter was as well, all because

Zionist Jews wanted to take my land in order to further the global, homosexual, multicultural enslavement and ultimate genocide of people that look like Jessica and myself.

It was nearing 1:00 am. She asked if we could sleep together. I couldn't be next to this woman and not be aroused. She noticed. My mattress was next to the window and the full moonlight allowed for some visibility in my room. We kissed passionately before she climbed onto me. She pulled her Victorian nightgown over her head and revealed those beautiful breasts. We took it slowly, not like that morning had been. I did my damndest to wait for her, but she was right with me the whole way. It was intense and ended as we clung tightly in a full embrace as I filled her again with my semen. She had tears again. But this time, I think they were tears of joy. We lay side by side. Before she fell asleep, she was rubbing my chest and feeling of my pectoral muscles.

She whispered softly, "You are strong." After that she stopped, and her muscles relaxed against me. As she slept, I envisioned us on a deserted island, on a beach in the sun...far away.

The next morning, I awoke to her rustling in my pantry. She saw me watching her and asked, "What do you eat for breakfast? I'll make it."

"Deer sausage and eggs. There's deer in the outdoor freezer, eggs in the mini fridge." She busied herself with breakfast as I dressed and freshened up. We ate together and she informed me that she had a couple of commitments to keep today. We gathered a few of her things and before we started for the door, she took a curious look at Jesus standing there on the water with His hand outstretched to whomever was looking at the painting.

"Do you believe, Zach?"

"I do." I replied as I picked up her duffle bag. "When I read the Bible and see what is happening in real time...I have no doubts. Especially when I read the parts where Jesus condemned the Jews and the parts where Paul stated that they are contrary to all men. Tell you what," I put the duffle bag down and went to grab my Bible from my bookshelf, "Take this...it has my notes in it...take your time." She took it from my hand and held it to her as though she would protect it with her life. She slipped her pretty feet into her Muck boots, and we left.

As I dropped her off, she told me that she would be back tonight late if that was ok. She would drive her car. I told her to pack her car with whatever she wanted to bring...and as far as I was concerned, there was no reason for her to stay there in an empty house. She smiled that beautiful smile like a person does when they've fallen in love. I returned it. She kissed me quickly and then darted to her porch, turning to look at me before I pulled away.

On my way back to the cabin I had to contact someone in order to hear from Lia. I called Margie. Lia was actually home from school that day due to a belly ache. I honestly think she hated school because of the niggers and the furies and the all-out waste of time that even an elementary student can already pick up on. Margie said that Tiffany hadn't been herself lately and she was hoping I could tell her what was going on. I simply told her that I had noticed a change in her as well, but I was still trying to get to the bottom of it. Lia was there with her grandma, and I got to talk to her and tell her that I loved her. She said she loved me too. I went through town in order to stop at the post office and visit a backwoods lawyer friend in order to get help with my current fiasco, but his office had been boarded up. I got a message from Jessica out of the blue that read, "Mark got shanked in prison yesterday" Then a few moments later as I was trying to think of how to respond, another text came through

24

from her. "LOL" It gave me the impression that she had zero feelings for what happened to him. Our conversation from the previous night convinced me of that. I simply replied, "Good for him, lol." I passed by the courthouse and saw Delwin's truck at the Commonwealth attorney's office. I also saw the Mazda of the judge whose son gang raped Jessica with help from Delwin. It occurred to me then and there that my hometown needed a purge. I was not born a violent man, and will seek peace when I can, but sometimes mercy comes for the innocent only when evil is removed, and sometimes God uses the hand of His people to take His vengeance. Putting that aside for now, I drove back to the cabin with a plan in mind and I hoped I could get it done before Jessica returned. I pulled up the floorboards that covered my secret stash of weaponry. I had quite an arsenal, more than one man could use efficiently, so I grabbed a couple of small caliber rifles that I knew were somewhat pricey and, with no reluctance, I loaded them in the truck. It was an hour's drive to the next biggest town, but I didn't need anyone locally finding out or even seeing me as I traded the guns off for money to purchase rings.

As I neared the city limits of Murrie, I saw the first Billboard sign with drag queen faggots on it. It read, "y'all, means ALL." I felt nauseous. I drove to a place in what I had hoped was the best side of town but street walking niggers, Guatemalans, and an all-out arrangement of foreign people were everywhere. I drove to another place and stopped for gas and placed a sticker above the pump that read: "Deport the Jews." Instead of looking for pawn shops, I decided to ask the White clerk if there were any gun stores nearby. He directed me to a place about 4 miles from there on the way out of town called Dan's Guns. I don't know if it was my look or just a hunch, but the man said, "It's your kinda place." I took that as a compliment.

25

As I entered, I had to agree with the clerk. They readily bought both my rifles and put enough in my pocket to buy what I needed. While at the counter, I noticed a newsletter near the register. It was like an old newspaper and was named "The Redoubt News." The owner saw me looking and said, "Bunch of people already left this town and gonna be a bunch more leave."

"Where are they going?" I asked.

"Some are going to Tennessee, some to Arkansas, some all the way to Idaho is what I hear."

I picked it up, "How much for this newsletter?" I asked.

"It's free." he replied. "Everyone is tired'a this shit! They rape young girls and get away with it in this town, and if you speak up about it or even try to defend yourself, ya get called racist or they might even put you in jail...Everybody that comes in here is looking for a way to get somewhere where a local government will stand up to these bastards and thumb their nose to big money they shell out to buy our officials off with. I got a list of places that might be promising if you're interested." "Yeah" I said as I looked up from scanning the pages. He left and returned momentarily with a printout of locations and contacts of people who were interested in getting out of this Jew dominated, flailing society. He added, "By the way, there is a vetting process so if you're a fucking FED, you ain't getting in... just so you know." This was interesting news to me. I gladly took the information in hand and heart.

I had already seen a Jewelry store and backtracked to go get what I came for. I was feeling my usual out-of-control feelings, wondering if I was making a wise decision. Everything was happening so fast. It wasn't just the relationship with Jessica that was moving at Mach 2, but it seemed everything was happening at

26

lightning speed, all at once. I did know that the feelings I had for her were real and nearly unstoppable. I took my time. I realized that I was going to have to guess at the size, but I estimated as close as I could and figured I could get it sized later. It was modest but pretty. I was confident enough to go ahead and buy the bands, so I bought the matching Celtic Cross set. The travel time afforded me the opportunity of thought. What was I willing to do? Life could not continue for me in this place. If I did not act at all, I would be jailed or thrown off my land or dead. What was going to happen to my daughter? Was she going to be raised thinking her dad was a 'mean ole racist' and had to be removed for the betterment of society? What were Tiffany's plans? I thought of how in my heart I just really wanted to be left alone to live my simple life and Jessica was the one I wanted to share that with. I resolved to look at every option and take life as it came and never turn my back on my faith or my family. I could never leave Lia.

I got back to the cabin after dark but early enough for me to do some serious research. I found out that Globaleyes was a mining corporation that found strands of lithium under the soil in and around the county and surrounding counties of my hometown. The migrant housing was just a ruse for those sympathetic Judeo-Christians to garner support. The Jews only care about migrants in the aspect of their ability to harm and displace or murder Whites. Bringing migrants to a town and not providing them with anything makes the situation ten times worse and that's what they intend. They will also accept third world working conditions and be praised as contributors to society because the Whites are succumbing to the drug crisis brought to them by the CIA and FBI. I also found that in the event that any resistance to the Corporations or any attacks on Federally protected migrants should happen, they would be met with force through 'peacekeeping military contracts,' which I perceived as U.N. troops or similar. I wondered how close we were at that very moment.

I looked at the list of contacts that Dan had given me at the gun shop earlier. There were nine altogether but only three that were realistic for what I was willing to do. I called the number to a man in Tennessee whose only name given was Wes. When the call went through, the man answered and asked who was speaking. With reluctance, I gave only my first name and tried to briefly explain why I was calling. Wes sort of cut me off and informed me that if I had gotten this number then he already knew what I wanted. He asked me a few questions that I thought were ridiculous, but he was likely listening for voice tones and signals that might alert him of someone who might be lying. After that he said that conversations cannot be made over the phone or through texts. He asked me if I was familiar with a small town in Tennessee named Fern Grove. I wasn't, but I could find out how to get there. "There is no commitment" he explained, "until the choice to fully commit to the future of the White Aryan race is made by you. Then you will call and be given directions to a location where you will be met by members of our Society. Once the call is made, you will discard your phone and any device that can be tracked. You are welcome to bring supplies, weapons and anything that will help further your relocation but if you arrive with any tracking device, you'll be disposed of immediately."

"What about housing and facilities?" I asked. I was put off initially by the coldness of his speech but at the same time I understood the precautions that must be taken to ensure the safety of those he was willing to protect. I wanted this structure and control over who might live next to me as well. I still needed more information in case this was what I had to eventually do. I could at least prepare those who might go with me. His reply was, "Zachary, any relocation is difficult; however, you will find that the people in Fern Grove have the same desires as you. They want a better world for their children, and helping you succeed is in their best interests. You will need to leave your old mindset of capital gain and dog-eat-dog financial competition behind you. Your skills will be put to work here and will be appreciated by those who benefit. In the end if you choose to go back to Babylon, you will be free to do so." He might have sold me on the whole concept with his last phrase.

I heard Jessica's car pull up. She was loaded down with belongings, so I assumed she never meant to go back to her house. We stacked her stuff on my floor. She also had an AK47 and several cans of ammunition for it. "It was Mark's. He had it in a storage container under my name. Some deputy gave an inmate in his cell his legal paperwork while Mark slept. It took about fifteen minutes for the deputies to respond to all the commotion...he was dead before they got him out of the cell." I was speechless. We stood in the light of my kitchen area and after a pause and an embrace she said, "I have something else to show you." She was dressed this time in jeans and her muck boots. She had on a green sweater under her camouflage coat and her hair was down in its beautiful, messy, waving style. She removed her coat and began to raise her shirt. I was fine with more sex. I would give her all she needed and in my mind that's what I fully expected to happen, but as she pulled her sweater over her head, she had on a strapless bra and was bandaged above her right breast.

"What the hell?" came out of my mouth, "Are you ok?" She grinned and I was totally confused. She began to remove the bandage tape from the corners. As she peeled away the packing, I saw it. A German Eagle holding that emblem of our people which the world has been taught to hate. She looked for approval in my eyes and she found it. It was identical to mine.

29

"I am yours Zachary Wayne Severs. I want to always be yours. I want to go where you go. I don't want to be apart from you." It was as if she was giving me her marriage vows. I reached for my coat, which was hanging on a nail, took the ring from the pocket and then from its casket. She gasped and cried and kissed me before I could even say a word. When she calmed down, I got on one knee and asked her properly. The ring fit perfectly. The evening ultimately ended as I thought it would. I was gentle but made her look at me with eyes open as we climaxed together.

I informed her of all I had found out that day. She agreed with me that if it were not for the fact that I would be leaving Lia behind, a calculated move might be in both our interest. We discussed every possible scenario and agreed that life would probably not wind up happening like we imagined it would at all, but we vowed to stay together no matter what. She told me her life prior to me had been full of self-harm, some drug use, pornography consumption, and depression. She was tired of sitting alone in her house waiting for something to change the elements controlling her existence. She hadn't ever really considered suicide, but she admitted to having some thoughts about how it wouldn't matter if she was dead, because no one cared. Her old life meant nothing, and she was ready to live for a new purpose. We read from the Prophets of the Old Testament before we went to bed, and she listened carefully to me as I explained the stories of our ancient people. She was more than interested. I don't think she had ever thought a lot about the world around her and how much the scripture related to the things happening in the world that she could see with her own eyes. We didn't stand before a preacher that night, but in our hearts, we were married just the same.

I awoke just a few hours later at 2:00 am, to the faint smell of wood smoke…which wasn't necessarily alarming because I had to use pipe cement to keep the flu from an occasional leak, but when I looked in the stove, the fire was out. I put my jeans on and my coat, "Where are you going?" Jessica asked sleepily.

"You smell that?" I asked.

"Something on fire?" she asked inquisitively.

"I'll be right back…" I could see the light as I ran up to the crest of the hill which let me look down into the valley of my property. The right-hand side had county road frontage that spanned nearly three acres and there was a bridge there that covered the creek splitting my property into basically two sections. It appeared that near the bridge there was an enormous fire I knew immediately that it must have been set and accelerated by someone because it was too wet for any natural occurrence to happen. I heard the fire trucks and police off in the distance. I headed back to the cabin with my phone in hand to call and let the fire department know that I was aware of it but that I had no idea how it started. Jessica was standing on the porch with her arms crossed in her long white nightgown and bare feet.

"Are they literally trying to burn you out of your home, Zach?"

"Looks like something pretty crazy is going on, doesn't it?" I replied. She waited as I called and was forwarded to dispatch. The lady on the line informed me that they received a call about ten minutes ago and that they assumed it was me who initially reported the fire. It had even been logged that I had called.

I was feeling that our lives may very well have been in danger at that point. I asked Jessica if anyone knew that she was staying with me and she said that she had only told her mother, who lived an hour away but was also on good family terms with Margie. It occurred to me that it was possible for Tiffany to have known that I had slept with her cousin, but that didn't bother me, but I was wondering if anyone would know to look for me at Jessica's house in town.

As the fire raged through the night, we packed my truck with as much as we could, with sirens screaming in the distance. She followed me in her car back to her house as the sun rose on a cold January morning. I pulled into the shed to shield my truck from easy viewing, and we carried in only what we might need for the next few hours. We got some coffee, and we put some ointment on her tattoo and rebandaged it. I knew for years to come I could never look at her without remembering her devotion to me.

Jessica got a call from her mother. She took it but I only heard one side of the conversation. "Yeah, we are together right now." There was a long pause, as Jessica listened intently to her mother's voice on the phone and then Jessica looked right at me with fear in her eyes and said, "Oh...My...God."

Tiffany was a beautiful teenager. She was on the cross-country team and was a cheerleader and very athletic. She had a picture-perfect smile and was envied by all who knew her. She was sociable and friendly and for the most part, kind to everyone she met. I remember the first time we had sex during our junior year, and we were so afraid that she might become pregnant. It was only later that we found out that she had some difficulty getting pregnant, which made the birth of our daughter Lia somewhat of a surprise after we had been married for four years. Life did not continue in the direction she wanted. Her life to that point held no disappointment and I believe it was her desire for life to continue in that fashion that pulled her away from reality with me into a delusion of money and ease.

Her body was found at the bridge near my house, partially burned, her throat sliced, and she was naked from the waist down and her hands restrained behind her.

Jessica dry-heaved and held her mouth and stomach. I closed my eyes and exhaled deeply and stood to hold her. Neither of us wanted this to happen. In both of our minds, Tiffany was still very much family. In an attempt to act before I allowed myself any grief, I calmly instructed Jessica to ask if Margie and Lia were aware of it. She said yes. Jessica agreed to call Margie because any calls she received would likely be monitored. Her husband Bill, who was Tiffany's stepfather, answered and said that Margie was unable to talk due to her emotional state. He did say that Lia was there, and safe and that Tiffany's husband Anthony was also there. He said the police were asking about my whereabouts. Evidently, they had just missed me. I couldn't imagine the story that was about to unfold. I knew I was never going back to my Granddad's farm. I would never see my cabin again. I knew what was in the truck was all the earthly possessions I had, and I also knew what I needed to do. I pulled Wes's number up on my contacts and showed the screen to Jessica.

"If we can get Lia..." I stated.

She nodded. "I'll get her...you make the call."

I was not in favor of letting Jessica go alone but we both knew if she was seen with me, it would be the end for both of us. She changed rapidly into her jeans and sweatshirt, put her hair in a bun, kissed me and went out the door. I had no knowledge of her plan, but somehow, she seemed to be very confident and fearless. I had faith that she would be back soon.

I made the call to Wes. I was instructed to go to a farm near the neighboring county line in which Fern Grove was the county seat. I was to turn off County Rd. 1380 onto Ivy Hollow Rd. At 1.8 miles, I was to park our car at a wide spot in the road and someone would meet us there. I was given an allotment of times to choose from, and since our destination was only five hours from my town of Silver Springs, I chose noon the following day. I only hoped I could avoid being arrested until then.

I tried to shower and mostly cried. I hadn't cried due to loss, since my mother died. I had never had such a flood of contradictory emotions in my life. I was literally still in the process of falling in love with Jessica and was now forced to deal with a grief I could not have imagined. The hot water from the shower nearly put me in a trance as my mind flashed memory after memory in front of me, of all the happy times Tiffany and I had had. If I could avenge her murder at some future point, I wouldn't hesitate.

I got dressed and turned on the local news in hopes of getting some information. It was worse than I thought. They had my flags on display. Cops were swarming my cabin with camera crews and police everywhere. I even saw Delwin in one frame as they showed the floorboards and arsenal I had tucked away. They were interviewing people I had never met, claiming to know me, talking about how I was a threat to society and evidently a murderer who would stop at nothing to further my White Supremacist ideology. Our negro police chief insured the 'fearful' public that they would catch me and bring me to justice for my ex-wife's brutal murder. In short, I was being framed and would likely never even stand trial in the anti-White courts.

I heard Jessica's car outside and I looked impatiently to see if Lia was with her. She was, thank God. She ran to hug me, and it was obvious that she knew something was wrong, but I was certain she didn't know the details.

"I told them I would take her to get ice cream, so we don't have long before someone might get suspicious." She said. Margie was distraught but Jessica said when she asked her secretly what she thought happened, all she could say was, "Zach didn't do this." It gave me relief to know that Margie knew me well enough to know I wouldn't hurt Tiffany for anything in the world.

"Did you call?"

"Yes, we will meet tomorrow at noon"

"Where are we going daddy?" Lia asked.

"We are going on an adventure" I said calmly. "I think you are going to have lots of fun..." I giggled.

Jessica smiled. "Guess what," she said to Lia, "I have some old Barbie dolls that I bet you might like...you want to see them?"

"Yes!" Lia exclaimed.

We all chuckled. Lia would turn eight this year. When Lia was settled in the other room, we discussed our plan and agreed to leave at dark. She told me that Delwin was pulling into the drive at Margie's as she was leaving with Lia. She wasn't sure but she thought he might have seen Lia.

"I know he saw me because he peered hatefully into my window to confirm to himself it was me. It won't take him long to put things together." Jessica said.

We loaded enough to get us to Tennessee in her car. My truck was obviously out the question as far as travel was concerned. I noticed as we were loading things up, that Jessica had a .38 Ruger tucked in her waistband. As her shirt rode up, I saw how her jeans desperately clung to her hips. Her figure and her feminine attributes were so distracting, and she was aware that her looks often caused me to lose concentration. I never asked about the pistol, but the idea that she knew how to use one gave me comfort that she was confident enough to use it for protection, so I let it pass from my thoughts. I had my Glock .45 as well and two other rifles besides the AK that Jessica had brought to the cabin the night before. We needed to ditch our phones somewhere really soon, but we couldn't leave them at Jessica's house because if they found it, she would be an accomplice, which was likely to happen anyway, and she knew it.

After resetting my phone to factory settings, I tossed it out the window a few miles out of town. We had to get somewhere we wouldn't be seen by those who knew us, so we drove to the small community called Hatchet. There were good country people there. There was a small park, a Church and a historic cemetery. We were not as well-known there as we were back in Silver Springs, but we didn't interact with anyone. We brought food with us from Jessica's and ate on a bench while Lia was swinging and playing on the playground. It was peaceful there. I walked through the cemetery, and I saw a few gravestones with my family name Severs... distant relatives, I was sure. One stone in particular caught my eye. The name on the stone was barely legible but I traced the lines with my finger and made out what appeared to be Volentine Severs. He had died in 1867 and was a young man. At the base of the grave was some sort of marker. I dug around in the dirt and unearthed an iron cross of valor. I wished, at that moment, my grandfather could see this and possibly explain who this man was to me. Even as a young child, my grandfather sowed the seeds of distrust for the Federal government. I always knew I had Confederate ancestors but I never knew any details. Jessica saw the last name which was a maiden name of her grandma who wasn't on Tiffany's side. We thought it very interesting that we would have ancestors in the same graveyard. It was also understood by us that we were both about to leave behind what had been home to our families for over a hundred and fifty years, or longer.

We left at dark. Jessica drove and I gave her directions to the town nearest Fern Grove. As we approached the county line, an unmarked vehicle pulled out behind us and turned its blue lights on. I was certain we were done for. Jessica was calm in the seat and pulled over to the curb on a straight stretch of road with harvested fields on both sides. I pulled my hat down low and turned to the window to make myself difficult to identify. It took a few moments and as Jessica rolled her window down, to our surprise...it was Delwin. He began chuckling before he said, "Well, well... what have I come across here?" in his utmost arrogant way. He was busy thinking of his next insult when Jessica calmly whispered to Lia,

"Sweetie, cover your ears." She did so quickly. I thought she might be getting ready to give Delwin a good cussing and didn't want Lia to hear such foul words.

As Delwin continued, "I got me a whore and her murdering boyfriend."

He started again with his evil chuckle, but it was cut short by the hand of a woman who had more reasons than she needed. My ears rang. I will never forget the look in his eyes the millisecond before she opened his skull with her .38. It knocked him backward and he lay in the road. She yelled out the window, "You piece of shit mother fucker." She shot twice more into his lifeless body. "You little-dicked son of a bitch." Maybe she did mean for Lia to not hear the foul language. She tossed the pistol on the dash and sped away as though nothing was the matter or that we had experienced anything unusual. We sat in silence for a long time. At some point thru the night drive, I heard her sing in a lowly angelic voice, "I put a golden band, on the right left hand this time." I knew that if we could be allowed, by the grace of God, to have any sort of future, Jessica, Lia and I, would make a life worth living. We just needed a chance.

We got a cheap motel in the town of Berryville at about 10:00 pm. We unloaded for the night and took her empty car a few streets down and left it in a lot with a few other cars, but not before I switched the plates. We walked back to the motel. There was not much sign of degeneracy or third worldliness around that I could see. There wasn't graffiti or trash overflowing in the street and the houses looked somewhat clean and cared for. I felt bad for switching the plates in that neighborhood, but I couldn't risk our safety. We got little sleep that night. After Lia fell asleep, we turned on the television to see what was being said about us. It was quite amazing how the media can portray an event. Jessica and I sat in pure wonder at the story being told. They had recovered Delwin's body of course and were busy turning him into a martyr. Jessica was named as an accomplice and somehow, they portrayed me as the leader of a local neo-Nazi terrorist organization. They said that the "family" was offering a reward for Lia's return. They really fixed the story well. There was now a nationwide manhunt for both of us. I knew in my mind that Tiffany had probably been killed by Delwin or murdered on his orders. I think Jessica thought so too. Even if he didn't, he still needed killing.

We lay in bed together. Any lights outside, voices, or any noise kept me paranoid and Jessica looked at me with those eyes which seemed to read my mind. Her hands caressed my chest and then wandered; my mind was everywhere but she brought me to the present. We were definitely anxious about our new life and although Jessica seemed to prove herself over and over to be more than a capable companion, she still needed my confidence, and my assurance we were doing the best possible thing. I think she also understood our choices were somewhat being made for us.

I had the directions to Ivy Hollow in my head. We had to go back to the bypass road and travel south for two miles until we came to 1380. Then west on 1380 for 6.3 miles and our road was on the right.

I recalled Wes saying that when I had decided to devote my life to the future of the Aryan race, I could make that call. I think at that time I was ready, even though I had been forced into it. I had already lived a life of watching my race wallow in the mud and take the oppression of foreigners as they steam rolled our towns, took our jobs, raped and assaulted our women. I was ready for a change even if it was drastic, as long as Jessica was beside me.

The next day I went to get the car. The vehicle that I switched plates with was already gone and a few different cars were parked in other spots. No one was around and I watched the area from a distance for a long while before going to get it. Back at the motel, we loaded our things and left at about 11:00 am to drive the short distance but I wanted to make sure we had no time issues in finding Ivy Hollow.

We turned onto 1380, and I have to admit I was somewhat nervous as was Jessica, but we didn't allow our anxiety to get in the way of our actions or let it be known to Lia. I wanted her to feel completely safe and secure. As Ivy Hollow Rd. came into view, Jessica and I gave each other a glance. I was driving and I slowed down as we turned in. We had 1.8 miles to go until we reached the complete uncertainty of our new life. I was concerned that the people in Fern Grove would know by now who I was, and I could possibly be turned over to the authorities. Jessica kissed me and lingered at my lips for a few moments before refraining herself. We didn't speak. I drove to the pull-off spot where I was instructed, and we were about 45 minutes early. It was a high wooded area.

We sat waiting and wondering. I tried to answer all of Lia's questions as much as possible, but I didn't have all the answers I wanted. Jessica knew I was trying my best. She grinned at me and said, "You are such a wonderful dad."

We finally began to hear gravel popping on the road. They came from both directions. Black SUVs with a total of ten men armed with military grade weapons. They stepped from the vehicles and formed semicircles around Jessica's car all the while having their rifles trained on us. It was a tense moment, and I was wondering what could possibly be happening. Lia started to cry, and Jessica tried to console her as I tried to explain who we were and what we were doing there. One of the men from the vehicle facing us said in a deep voice, "Don't talk."

No sooner than he said those words, a frail older gentleman slowly stepped out of the passenger side. He moved with slowness and a gait that suggested arthritic pain was a constant battle for him. His skin was weathered brown, a look that an Aryan man has when he is in the sun for most of his life. He was dressed in a brown Sunday suit. He moved towards us slowly, looking at us through his glasses. Jessica and I glanced at each other and then back at the old man. When he got within 5 yards he stopped.

"Your name is Zachary Wayne Severs, Is that correct?" He

cleared his throat.

"Yes Sir" I said.

"Is this your family?"

"Yes Sir"

This was not Wes. Wes sounded much younger.

"Zachary…" he paused with the inflection that he had more to say, and I dared not interrupt him. "...You understand that we take every precaution here..." He coughed some more, "You and your family have nothing to fear if your intentions are pure...if they are not pure, then we will find out soon and you will be..." he glanced at Lia and refrained from the harshness of his speech that he might have delivered had she not been there, "...well, let's just say you won't live here in Fern Grove."

"I understand totally."

"Good. My name is Elijah." He coughed again and pulled a rag from his back pocket to wipe his mouth. "You'll ride with me to our next stop, ...these gentlemen will bring your car along with your ...luggage.

Chapter 2

Arrival

What transpired in the next few hours were the turning points in both our lives. We had passed the point of no return and to me it felt as though we had given up our old lives completely. I felt a euphoric feeling and I could see Jessica during the entire process soaking up all available knowledge and making the very best of every possible situation and question they had for us. We could not see out of the SUV and were accompanied by men in front and behind us. They were probably not allowed to speak to us, so we rode in silence. We exited the vehicle in front of what appeared to be a remodeled three-story school building from a century ago, but inside it was very modern and updated nicely while leaving the historical touches of the large doors and moldings. At the entrance there were stairs. Instead of going up to the first-floor level, we descended into the basement. The whole building was bubbling with activity like you might see during a war time movie. People talking franticly and sharing information, but everyone there looked like us. White.

We entered a room and sat down. I understood this to be the vetting process. Two years from that date I would become part of the panel during this process, but that day, I was unprepared for what was next. Tiffany and I were taken one at a time and strip-searched to make sure we had no wires or devices or implants of any kind. Jessica's search was conducted by two other females who Jessica said even helped her rebandage her two-day old tattoo with genuine care. We were seated again together with Lia, and Elijah asked if we were interested in allowing Lia to go into a room adjacent to us, which was divided by glass, and be watched by the women assisting with the vetting process so that we could talk openly. I agreed. I had lots to tell these people, and I didn't need Lia to hear it, at all.

Jessica shocked me to some degree with her budding knowledge of what was really happening in the world, and some of the answers she gave to questions even made some of the men in the room chuckle with her short blunt replies. When asked if we were practicing any religion, Jessica blurted out quickly, before I could form the words, "We're Christian...not Judeo".

She looked at me as if to ask if she was right, and everyone in the room laughed, including myself. She eventually laughed too but mostly because we were laughing. Elijah spoke softly as the room reverenced anything he said, "You will make a wonderful addition to our community...most of our incoming families are the same." He cleared his throat.

I was wondering at what point we would have to discuss what had ultimately brought us to Fern Grove and the thought of sharing that with them scared the shit out of me. What caught me totally by surprise was that everyone in the room had been briefed on who I was before they even met us at Ivy Hollow. They knew by watching the news that I was being framed. They did want to hear my version and before I ended talking about it, Jessica and I were both nearly in tears. She held onto my arm and laid her head on my shoulder as I did my best to explain in as much detail as I possibly could.

Many of the people in Fern Grove were or had been in similar circumstances and, to my surprise, they basically had a network that operated much the same as a witness protection program. What really amazed me was that they had so much organization and infrastructure built up and I was living alone, scared of society, in my little cabin in the woods. What really made me feel like we had made the greatest choice we could make was when they rolled a television set into the room and began playing a video that at first, I did not recognize at all, and then I heard the voice of an irate young gentleman in front of a crowd at a library. It was the library at Silver Springs, and the young gentleman was me. Jessica lifted her head off my shoulders in an attempt to shake herself as if to see if what she was seeing was real. I could tell she looked at me briefly to see my expression, but I was in total shock. The speech I gave that day was an impromptu speech directed at the county officials and parents of Silver Springs who had gathered in the parking lot to facilitate a drag queen parade. I remember being livid that day and I certainly had no idea anyone recorded it, nor did I have any clue how these good people had obtained it. I couldn't remember everything I said that day, but when hearing it again, I certainly still felt the same way and would never apologize for it even if it meant my life. As the police began to drag me from the library steps, the man who brought the monitor stopped the video. There was silence in the room.

Elijah finally spoke, "If the man...in that video still exists..." He coughed terribly and had to regain his strength of speech "...then we want him and those who love him ...to be a part of the world we are going to create for our children and grandchildren."

"He's alive and well, Sir" I said proudly.

Jessica looked at me and grinned.

Elijah summoned one of the men with a simple nod. The man stepped out only momentarily and returned with an ancient looking

Bible. Its spine was cracked, and the leather was worn and dirty. It was placed in front of me and Jessica.

"Let's all stand", Elijah spoke with an anointing, even with simple words. We stood.

"Four years ago...when we began this journey..." He coughed and cleared his throat, ".... we found this Bible in the basement here in this building. Many names of the founding members of this community are recorded inside..." His accent was very plain Southern. "We hold the same beliefs about freedom that they did. We have no desire to restrict those freedoms from you here. You will find in fact, the avenues available to you here that will allow you to be active in protecting those freedoms in the ways that you have likely longed for in your heart." Cleared his throat again and paused... "If you are ready Zachary and Jessica, place your right hands on the Book.... and repeat after me."

We were somewhat in awe of our surroundings for the next few days and weeks to come. After we were administered the oath, the men and women there in the room lost their coldness and warmed to us. All our fears subsided, and we were allowed to talk casually with people who were just like us in mind and spirit. I was given a copy of the Oath to place in my own Bible. It read...

"I, Zachary Wayne Severs, with the knowledge that the White Aryan peoples of the earth are under an unprecedented attack on their lives, and the lives of their children, do solemnly swear, that with unmeasured faith, I will act in accordance with the laws of God and in devotion towards His people which are my brethren. I will commit the remainder of my life to the common goal of securing a future for our race, hand in hand with those who have taken this same Oath... So Help Me God. The One God of Abraham, Issac, and

Jacob. In the Holy Name of Jesus Christ, Amen."

We were shown to a small three-room cottage at the edge of town and were assured that we would be safe. Jessica's car was in the drive and our luggage untouched. We were ecstatic. Jessica went to work immediately to make it feel like home. I still had questions about all of the details about life there and how things were paid for and things of that nature. The first night was full of peaceful rest for both of us and Lia, but we were scheduled to be back at the Old School house for some informational meetings and some classes that all new arrivals at Fern Grove must take.

How I was unaware that this type of resistance to the Jew-dominated society existed was beyond me. Under Elijah's direction, what had started as a single act of resistance against a fraudulent election, blossomed into a network of White Christian retaliation, not only in Fern Grove but in the surrounding communities as well. Little by little, the movement had gained speed and become equipped with an entire intelligence agency that worked to combat the anti-White Global Agenda at every turn. I had even learned that Elijah had my name on his radar before Dan at the gun shop had forwarded my information. Wes, who I finally met, was expecting my call that night.

I was placed with a team of builders at the beginning of our first week. The team was in charge of building homes for newcomers and also did maintenance on the public buildings. We ate in town together where all our wives gathered to prepare our lunches. Jessica never complained one time. I left in the mornings early, knowing I would see her at lunch. As I returned home in the afternoons, there were always scheduled community events that allowed for fellowship with the people there and we attended communal festivals and feasts and also participated in the setup of such events. During the Spring festival, which lasted several days, there was a gathering at the square near the old Courthouse which became a social event for the families to fellowship and get better acquainted with each other. There was a new pavilion on the lawn and hundreds of locals came to eat, drink, and dance into the night. This was not like events I had been to in the past but this was something that probed my genetic memory. There were men with banjos and fiddles. Guitar players and flutes. One man wore a kilt and played 'Scotland the Brave' on bagpipes. He received the largest applause of the night. We were introduced to several families. I tried being present in my conversations with all the men I talked to, but I could not help but overhear a few of the questions that were being asked of Jessica, about how we arrived at Fern Grove. One woman hinted vaguely about the rumors among them as to whether she had killed a police officer in order to get out of the town where we came from. Jessica didn't really know how to answer and I could see how uncomfortable she felt even though the ladies held her actions in very high esteem. She had almost arrived in Fern Grove with celebrity status and her beauty only added to her intrigue.

A man named Matt, who was near my age or older, seemed reserved and confident. He waited for others to have the opportunity to talk and then, as the crowd around us slightly abated, he approached me and introduced himself. He had been present the day on the road at Ivy Hill and also during the vetting process but he wanted to properly introduce himself. He was a Fern Grove native. He went to high school there and he and his wife, Laura, had lived in the local area their entire lives. He asked if I would be interested in doing some hunting. He provided lots of the meat for smoking during the festivals and wondered if I liked to hunt. He also talked about the decline in morality and his desire to change the world in

47

any way, big or small for his children. So many opportunities that my generation took for granted were no longer available to our children. We shared similar views on nearly everything and I felt a comradery with Matt from the get-go. His full name was Matthew Adelson Clarke and he informed me that Adelson was the name given him, after his Great-Great Grandfather. His family name came from Alabama but they settled in Tennessee sometime after the War. Whenever someone in the south refers to 'the War', they only mean one war in particular and anyone they are speaking to should know which war that is. In Southerners' minds, there was only really one war in the history of America and they are still fighting it. I believed in my mind, I was still fighting it as well because when Matt spoke about the 'War', I knew exactly what he meant.

Jessica and I were taken completely off-guard when the makeshift coordinator called for the new couple from Silver Springs to make their way to centerstage as the fiddler began to play a slow lullaby that filled the night air with a romanticism I never knew before. We were reluctant and neither of us relished being in the limelight, but knew there was no way to gracefully decline; so, she took my hand and I lead her to the floor as the other couples moved to the sides. We looked into each other's eyes as we began to slowly and somewhat awkwardly move to the melodramatic sounds. I whispered to her that she was a strikingly beautiful woman. She smiled and blushed because she knew I was telling her the truth. The light on her face, the smells of wood smoke, and the small hint of wine on her lips almost made me feel as though we had entered into a fairytale land. I never questioned our decision to come to Fern Grove after that. The crowd cheered loudly as the music ended and we bowed as if we were the main attraction. I saw Matt and Laura clapping and smiling with genuine feelings of happiness for us. I had never felt a feeling so authentic and true coming from my peers.

These people wanted everyone around them to succeed, and they loved their own. That much was obvious.

We lived on a high for a few weeks with all the positivity surrounding our arrival at Fern Grove. Lia had enrolled in the country Christian school not far from our cottage and Jessica took her every morning and she would talk about her friends and teachers at supper each night. After Lia was asleep, we continued our frantic lovemaking, and the world seemed to be passing like a dream. One afternoon when I returned home, Jessica met me at the steps of our cottage with a huge smile on her face.

"Guess what?"

"What?" I smiled.

"Guess!" she said demandingly.

About that time, Lia came through the door and hugged me around my waist.

"What if it's a boy, daddy? What are we gonna name him?"

I looked with wide eyes at Jessica to get confirmation and she nodded and smiled. I picked her up off her feet and held her and kissed her.

Chapter 3

Resistance Begins

It occurred to me in the coming months that our blissful new life was not going to continue without sacrifice. Some of the guys who were builders with me had become close friends. I was allowed to hunt with them and our families grew close. Lia played with their children, and we even began going to home bible studies with them regularly. I had always had a knack for public speaking and was eventually chosen to lead the studies. I had a unique ability to rally the hearts of men and women, and it quickly became apparent that I may need to pursue some sort of position in the future with that in mind. The immediate future, however, was being formed by my prowess in the hunting and marksmanship areas of my life. My friends began telling stories about shots I was able to pull off when hunting game and I will admit that some of them were exaggerations. None-the-less, I was becoming somewhat of a legend in the community.

Jessica supported me in every aspect of our lives there. She was prospering in every way as well. Spiritually, I had seen her grow exponentially. Her knowledge and faithfulness to God and the scriptures started to become apparent in her life. The foul language she was so fond of using in her past became relegated to our bedroom only. She spent some nights in a chair reading from the Bible I handed her months ago at my cabin. She was involved with the wives of my friends and together they cooked and canned vegetables. She learned how to knit and sew, and I was amazed at how she had adapted. Somewhere in both our minds, I think we knew that had we not come to Fern Grove, we would likely be dead.

About the time Jessica was entering her third trimester, I was asked to come to the Old School House. I was briefed before going into a meeting which included some of our highest, most revered men in Fern Grove, and what was about to be discussed was highly confidential. I learned that some people in the community were not completely privy to the goings on of the political structure at the high levels.

The intelligence agency had been named, The FGIA, for obvious reasons and after nearly five years in existence, they were prepared to no longer remain silent while the towns and communities in the immediate surrounding areas became victims of the orchestrated genocide of our people. A military operation was being planned, and training was being scheduled with ex U.S. military defectors who had sought refuge here at Fern Grove. The operation was going to consist of the removal of an installed city mayor of a town 45 minutes away who was openly gay and had brought busloads of degenerate people from the inner cities to parade in the quiet little town, even after the people had protested vehemently. The ZOG-bot police forces in these communities were worthless and the justice systems completely bought out. What was going to happen was a clandestine full-frontal night attack on the homes of the mayor and a very anti-White Judge, who was guilty of sentencing a young White female to jail time, after complaining online about her uncomfortableness in her hometown due to the frequent attacks by migrants. This had become a scene all too familiar. Whites everywhere were being threatened with fines and imprisonment if they did not submit and comply with their own rape and murder. My role in the process was to provide cover in the event that our men would come under fire from the ZOG police. My friend Matthew from the building team was going to cover the assault on the Judge and I would cover the one on the mayor.

I wanted to continue my peaceful life at Fern Grove, but I knew that the Global Agenda was not afraid of us, nor were they going to stop the slaughter of our people. In the years leading to my radicalization, I had watched the European countries be completely ravaged by Muslim invaders who were brought into the countries by Jewish organizations promoting ideas like human rights and help for refugees. Not one single mainstream channel ever followed the horrors that were happening to our ancient homelands. The only way to see how many rapes, stabbings, and beheadings were actually happening was to follow independent and alternative sources, which for normal Americans, was too much to ask. I never found a single person in my hometown of Silver Springs who felt angry at all about our own people across the ocean who were being subjected to some of the worst misrule in the history of White nations. I knew back then that it was a matter of time before the same things began happening in America. The brainwashing worked so well against our men that the safeguards our founding fathers put in place were never activated. Just like in Europe, when our daughters would get raped and murdered, the victims' fathers would take to the podium in their desperate attempt to convince the public that we should not let their child's murder cause anyone to have racist feelings against the migrant murderers. I saw this as a mental sickness. When the entire political system is corrupt, and even the local mayors and judges are willing to allow the destruction of their own people, violence is the only option left available. The White genocide machine was well oiled, and it had never been challenged thus far. That was about to change.

We were all reminded of our Oath and began training immediately, and my work was cut down to three days a week while the other two days were spent in training. I was given a military sniper .308 and trained regularly. I studied maps, escape routes, and 3D imaging of the terrain surrounding the mayor's home. We watched videos of city council meetings of the mayor making fun of and mocking his people and belittling them during public question and answer sessions. All of us hated him enough to follow through with his removal. We watched backroom videos of the judge, and we had been informed of the child pornography that he was involved in, and the rape of several boys and girls in his community, and the names of the deputies who were gladly taking payment to keep it all from public view. The information was that most of the people did know, however, and some of the talk I was hearing suggested that we had been invited to take care of the situation, or that we had at least been consulted on how to remedy it.

It was during our first year at Fern Grove that my first son was born. Jessica gave birth at home with the help of a midwife, and we agreed that his name would be Ephraim. He was two months old when the day came for us to follow thru with the assault. Naturally, Jessica did not want me to participate, and she did her best to hide her fear. I didn't give her the full details but assured her that my role in the event was likely the safest position I could have been chosen for.

We'd meet at noon the day before our operation. It would be carried out during the early hours of the following morning between 1:00 am and 1:30 am. We had every intention of being back safely in Fern Grove before 3:00 am and back in bed with our wives.

Each team had six men. Our transport was parked one mile from the mayor's house and the five men with me were men I knew very well. Our children played together, and our wives sang hymns together. If they needed me to pull the trigger on an entire police force to clear them an escape route, I was prepared to do so. I had never killed a man but was willing if the circumstance presented itself. I would have killed Delwin if Jessica hadn't so gloriously beaten me to it. I was also glad to be administering our own justice instead of always being on the receiving end of whatever bullshit the globalist Jews were force feeding us. It was finally time to send the message, loud and clear, that the anti-white communist regimes in these towns would not continue without resistance any longer.

I was on a slope about one hundred-fifty yards above the mayor's house. We climbed the cell tower and cut communication in that entire area. From my position, I could see the road coming in both directions and I could see the house where my brethren began approaching. There were nearby houses that made accomplishing our goal a bit chancy, but the alarm system was disabled by the cell tower disruption and one of our men cut electrical power to the house moments before they entered. The plan was to read both the mayor and the judge their crimes and how they had been sentenced to death. Then death would be administered quickly by silent means, (throat cutting).

I waited. I will admit that I was a little jealous of those who were getting to partake in administering the justice inside the house, but I knew that my job was just as important. The guys inside knew they could perform their jobs more efficiently knowing I had eyes and ears for them outside the house. I was hoping that at some point I would be able to change roles in a future mission. Only four of our men entered the home. The fifth man stayed in the shadows outside. I heard a small dog bark only twice and after that, our men exited the house in about five minutes. My orders were to wait until they were out of sight and moving in the direction of our transport vehicle, then move through the woods to a designated, secluded area to be picked up about ten minutes later. We never heard the first siren or commotion of any kind, and the operation was a complete success. When I jumped in the SUV, I was greeted by men, who like me, were driven by something deep. We weren't boys who had just pulled off toilet-papering our high school rivals' front yard, we were aging men who knew full well that this was likely only the beginning of a lifetime commitment to an all-out physical confrontation. Our crew leader was Jackson. His daughter was Lia's best friend. He had been in the FGIA since its conception, and he carried out the death sentence. He spoke the only words during the forty-five-minute commute back home.

"Killed that bastard's sodomite lover, too."

Jessica wasn't sleeping when I returned. She had been awake feeding Ephraim who was back asleep. We embraced, she clung to me, and we kissed passionately. She had recovered from giving birth very well and needed me to show her how much I still enjoyed her body. I obliged her. Our love had grown into a mature love, and we were of the same mind on nearly everything. She was beautiful in every way.

In the days that followed we heard rumors about how the news of the murders were circulating around the country. Our crews were brought to the Old School to view some of the main stream's coverage of our operation. It was typical Jewish propaganda. If all you watched was the MSM you would think that the people in that town loved their politicians and the bought-out police force as well. We also learned that as a result of our actions, a peacekeeping military installation was being brought in to keep the citizens 'safe'. We all snickered and shook our heads it was so laughable. We left that day with orders to return in two weeks to be briefed on another mission. This next mission would be further away, in Kentucky.

One of the most demoralizing pseudo-assaults against our

culture and way of life came in the form of the degenerate parades that mocked our values, insulted our heritage, and destroyed decency. The mayors and judges and police forces needed to be hung on the courthouse steps and everyone knew it. What I could never understand about our people is that they spent years hoarding guns and ammunition they had decided they would never use. In my eyes, the time for an all-out, grass roots uprising had seemingly come and gone. I remembered seeing the "Don't Tread on Me' stickers and flags waving from truck beds a few years back but where were they now? Our people had been more than 'tread on'. When the possibility of a project we called, "Raid on a Parade" was brought to my attention, I was anxious to find out the particulars.

We were going in as a team of snipers.

Thus far, there had been no serious physical threat to any parade and, therefore, we felt as though it was time to make the participants think twice before getting bused to a town they didn't know and acting like animals or worse. In several towns where the gay parades were carried out uncontested, there were naked men with collars being led on leashes by shirtless, feminine creatures who had scars where breasts had been. Not one single person had normal looking hair and some of them had metal in their noses and all over their skin. Some of these people were so depraved they would wear giant blow up vaginas or penises on their heads while they screamed their pronouns at each other and held signs promoting all kinds of filth.

There had been a church organization which had traveled from town to town to voice some peaceful opposition to the faggots, but as the sodomites flashed their genitals at the children, the church crew was threatened with arrest and removal. We counted on the church being there to take front and center as the sole opposition. As pathetic as it was, it lulled the ZOG-bots into a feeling of comfort. They felt no real fear from the church counter-rally.

We knew the fallout could be disastrous so we took precaution and did not proceed until we were confident we could reduce the police force dramatically at the outset of engagement. We also knew we might have to fight our way out of town, and we were prepared for that as well. After all the intelligence was gathered, and the plan developed, we delivered.

There was a large number of police on the day of the parade. ZOG always wants to make sure their sick agenda moves forward, and all the minds of the people corrupted. We had all stashed our rifles in areas which were accessible and, against our will, tried to blend in. I knew I looked ridiculous with the green-haired wig. We all did. I wore sporty shorts and t-shirt, because there was no way I was going to wear anything remotely like what I saw that day. The only thing we all had on which was remotely similar, were our boots. If I had to run, it was not going to be in sandals.

The parade would start at noon. The little country town did not deserve what was coming on this day, but its refusal to act in any way other than all-out compliance was the reason it had to take place. After we were done, no one would volunteer to be bused anywhere to take part in a homo-pedo parade.

As the parade came up the street toward us, it looked like the gates of hell had opened up and were about to flood the town. The church group began their insults almost immediately which led to a few minor altercations. Although I was of the opinion that the church's efforts were too little and too late, I was somewhat proud of them. It did take courage to stand there and take the abuse from the police and the sodomites. They were willing to be outnumbered and threatened and that was, at the least, commendable.

We all moved nonchalantly to our weapons as the distraction kept everyone's attention. My mini-AR was stashed in a hollow tree next to the commerce building. After I retrieved it, I ran up two flights of stairs and took position completely unnoticed as everyone was focused on the startling scenes below. My instructions were to take out as many of the police force as possible. My friend Matt was across the street from me and would work his way from the rear as I worked from the front of the parade down and as we met in the middle; we would scan the area for any would-be backup before retreating to our transport pick up location.

Before I shouldered my rifle, I took off my ludicrous hair piece. This was about to be a triumphant moment, and nothing could take away the glory of it like a green wig.

I waited for Matt as I sighted an overweight cop who was bullying a pedestrian, who evidently said something he didn't like. I heard Matt's rifle, and I let go a barrage of lead that rained down on the hired scum who oppressed our people. I lived in the moment. I was convinced that nothing would cease this take-over of our home until men finally decided that enough was enough. The street became a bloody nightmare. The proud, arrogant voices were silenced as they should be. The police were taken completely off guard and were not able to mount any sort of retaliation. Most of the police lay bleeding in the street along with the naked faggots they were sworn to protect, still wearing their dog masks and giant penises. Some of our men on the ground still fired intermittently as I scanned the area. I knew a few officers had run and were either hiding or about to come up the stairs. The window in the room next to me had a scaffold on the outside and I made a mental note I could use it if I had to. I still had at least 10 rounds left out of 30, and as I left the room, a negro officer along with a White officer pointed their pistols at me. The negro got off a round that didn't strike me, before I put him down. The White officer looked scared and dropped his pistol before putting his hands up. I almost shot him but something inside kept me from it. We looked into each other's eyes briefly, but I could tell he saw the disgust I had for him. He cried pitifully as I ran past him to the rear of the building. On the back stairwell, I had to shoot another officer who drew on me but after that, I ran freely.

All of us had rallying points consisting of five men. I was picked up at the water treatment facility about six blocks away with the others who were assigned that pick up. We waited for the fifth man to arrive but when the fourth came, he informed us we had a few casualties. Anytime there is a loss, it takes away some of the joy of victory, but we all knew the possibilities, and there was not one man among us who was not willing to sacrifice everything for the good of our future and the future of our children.

In the weeks to come, the U.N. installed a significant number of troops across the nation. There was chaos all across the states of Tennessee and Kentucky. There were violent migrant gangs overwhelming the cities and starting to move into suburban areas, and there was significant resistance from local communities, but they had no organization remotely close to the FGIA. Elijah had been spending time away from Fern Grove, and rumors trickled down that he was helping establish other groups across the state in hopes of aligning them with us to mount a larger offensive. Responsibilities trickled down. I began taking on larger and more time-consuming roles as we continued to grow in our projects and missions. I had begun to feel as though my life was no longer my own. I was guilty of letting my work consume me and I could tell that I was out of balance.

The night before our next mission into Kentucky, Jessica and I lay in bed quietly. If she had fears, she seldom allowed me to see. If she disagreed with me, she kept her silence. She was full of life and spunk, but when it came to me, she had settled in her heart to be submissive. I think she had wanted it before our first encounter, and it never changed during our lives together. She could tell I was bothered and looked at me with those understanding eyes of hers that had so totally seduced me over a year ago. She knew I needed to say something, but she didn't press me. She waited until I could form the words and then I said softly, "If you could have foreseen our lives now, would you still call and ask me for a load of wood?"

She looked at me and grinned. She lay her head on my chest before saying, "Sure, I would. I mean, I miss you when you work but I can busy myself here. There is enough purpose in our lives here that keeps me going, ...plus I would have missed out on getting spanked and fucked by the sexiest alpha male in Kentucky..." She caused us to nearly wake Ephraim with our laughter. We kept it low and then she said, "One thing you must always do for me..."

"Name it." I said.

With all seriousness, she replied, "Come home.... always come home to me."

Our team had evolved into a unit. We were charged with making an assault on the troops who had been deployed to put down a resistance in the town of Oxboro, some three and a half hours north of Fern Grove. Over the past several months, our men had been working tirelessly on preparing the plan. Our enemies were emboldening the migrant hordes to pillage from the rural and suburban Whites. The troops were being called upon to stop any uprising that was occurring due to violence against our people. In other words, they were only there to make sure that our genocide was conducted peacefully and without too much fuss from those being genocided. Reports of murders and rapes and even beheadings of rural farmers had brought us to this point. The world was out of control. I even wondered how long Fern Grove could isolate itself from the destruction.

We had explosive charges rigged to the pillars of an overpass that was the only route on which military convoys could travel in order to get to the disturbance we were going to create. Hotels and housing spots for incoming migrants in Oxboro were numerous. Some apartments were being constructed but had largely been abandoned. Our men were to cause a disturbance by setting fires, and possibly engaging the local police, in an attempt to draw out the troops who were within ten minutes of the migrant complex. Our unit consisted of fifty men, divided into two groups. One group would start the disturbance and engage the law enforcement, while the other sabotaged the troops as they attempted to answer the call for help.

We were spread across the top of a road that had been cut out years earlier. The overpass was about an eighth of a mile from me and when the charge blew, it would hopefully destroy at least some of their military vehicles and then stop the remaining convoy below us in a 'fish in a barrel' type situation. As far as having any sort of military genius or knowledge of ballistics and maneuvers, I am not highly skilled in any of these departments, but I have a knack for being somewhat cool under pressure and having a steady hand when it comes to marksmanship.

Several of the men in my group were again, close friends and men who I had developed a camaraderie with over the last year. We lay in silence for hours waiting for any word from the unit in town and whether or not they were following through with the mission accordingly. We were not able to hear any of the details. At about 10:00 pm we were advised to be ready. Some civilian traffic was continuing to pass through, unaware of our presence and the later it got, the less traffic there was. As I saw the first trucks come into view, I knew that the bomb crew was receiving their countdown from the top of the ridge across from me. I couldn't hear anything except trucks moving at a rapid speed, which I knew must be considered when deciding when detonation occurs. I was glad that this was not my department.

As the first truck came within mere yards of the overpass, the charges detonated. The sounds after that were horrendous, like an avalanche and tearing metal. Big booms could be heard for miles I'm sure but the screaming, as one of the trucks exploded, was drowned out with the noise of the blast. I heard some scattered gunfire near the bridge moments after the third truck barreled over onto two other trucks that could not stop in time to avoid going headlong over the collapsed bridge. There were vehicles resembling U.S. military grade, five-ton Deuce and a Half and some jeeps with mounted guns. We were instructed to wait until the troops exited the vehicles and were in the road. As they did so, I watched through my scope and decided to pick off the drivers and anyone who appeared to be in a leadership role. Anyone who was talking to other troops as if to give orders was going to get my bullet first. My shot was scheduled to initiate the others with me who would fire only after me, and then at will.

Two five-ton trucks stopped directly in front of me at what I guessed to be less than seventy yards, accounting for the downward flight travel. My rifle was flat shooting, and I had no lack of confidence in what I was about to perform. Men scrambled from the trucks and jeeps all over the road. There had to be at least one-hundred men or more on the road seconds after they came to a halt. The road lights and truck lights illuminated their faces well enough for me to see that none of these men were naturalized citizens. I could also hear indistinct chatter coming from them and it was not English. As I saw the first man direct a group of men, I silenced him. My bullet ripped through him and left the men at his command stunned as our men unleashed a hailstorm of rapid fire on those mongrel bastards. They scurried as some of them fell. They were taken completely off guard, and we shot them to pieces. Our men rushed into the road to finish off any of the wounded and we climbed aboard the jeeps and trucks as the bomb crew and their retreat coverage team made their way back to Fern Grove. We drove back to the nearest exit and took a scenic route into Oxboro.

According to our communications, our men there had suffered some casualties and had retreated into an abandoned garage and were basically trapped. We had to make decisions in real time because we had never encountered a trial of this proportion before. Matthew was with the crew in the garage and with the bomb crew gone, I was looked upon as being in charge. Everyone looked to me to decide our course of action. We were going to arrive and pose as help to the local law enforcement and assess on arrival if we would be able to take them with the munitions available to us. We stopped before entering town to see if we could man the turret guns on the jeeps. We had one ex-U.S. defector with us who could fire the weapon, and he quickly demonstrated his knowledge to a young man named Eric who was a fast learner with plenty of vigor for fighting.

As we saw the flashing lights, I only had a few seconds to view what we were working with and make a split decision that might affect the fate of all of us. Lines of cop cars and military police force equipment lined up in a double row providing cover from a dilapidated building that looked like hell. I told our men to radio that we were going to drive right into them and open fire, causing as many casualties and as much damage as possible and do it quickly. Then, get our men out of the trap they were in and load everyone into the two five-ton trucks. I smashed the Deuce into a police car and Eric and Walter began unloading on them from close range. They were so stunned that they were unable to return fire. The boys in the two five-tons were busy loading our comrades and our wounded while we continued our unholy barrage of gunfire on these traitors in uniform. We dealt them a devastating; humiliating blow and we left the jeeps and the Deuce in rubble behind us. The fires that our boys had set at the migrant complex were still burning out of control. They had done a wonderful job in spite of the setback they encountered. We were successful beyond measure, but the taste of blood only whetted our appetite for the long road ahead.

When we returned to Fern Grove I was hailed as a hero. The men made sure everyone knew I was responsible for the actions taken to retrieve our men from the garage. I didn't want any attention, nor was I interested in moving into any type of authoritative position, but it seemed inevitable. Some of our leaders had moved on to take positions in communities across the U.S. Vacancies needed to be filled and along with those vacant positions came housing. My family was growing, and I wanted the best for them even if it might be for a short time. We moved into a three-bedroom brick home, not far from the Old School. Jessica was given the opportunity to create a home in ways she had never experienced. She busied herself tirelessly every day and Lia grew during that time and began to blossom.

When asked by the FGIA if I would lead a mission into the town of Silver Springs, I jumped at the opportunity. The town was flooded with migrants and NGO's orchestrating their relocation by uprooting the White families who had lived there for centuries. They knew I had a vested interest in the town and would be interested in being part of a show of resistance. It was a risky undertaking. It was a far travel distance, and the job required sniper abilities and survival instincts to keep alive until I could be picked up. The plan was to put fear into the minds of the individuals who were getting paid by the ZOG government to betray their own race and people. When faced with an enemy or a traitor, the traitor is more dangerous because he goes about his treachery unnoticed.

The migrant housing complexes were quite elaborate, and drivers were transporting buses of Haitian and Somalian invaders to wherever they needed to go. Tiffany's widower didn't seem to have a problem moving on after her death. He was living in a gated community free from the fear of machete wielding savages. When he was not in Silver Springs, he was flying to the Bahamas or to Hawaii with his new Zionist girlfriend.

I was given a transport team who would pick me up six hours after the strike. We agreed on a time frame that I set due to my knowledge of the terrain. They would also detonate an explosive device planted near the police station moments after my shots. This would hopefully provide enough confusion to buy us some time. The high area from which I would conduct my mission was familiar to me. It was somewhat difficult to be in the general area again as it brought back negative feelings. I resolved to treat the mission as I would any other and tried to remain focused on the bigger picture and not on my own personal revenge. This was not an overnight operation. I stayed in the woods above the town for nearly a week while remaining in contact with the transport team as they roamed freely throughout the town, gathering information and clues for me about the whereabouts of the NGO President and arrival times of incoming migrants. There was ample evidence everywhere that nobody in the town of Silver Springs were willing participants of the multicultural experiment. From the ridge above town, I was able to witness gangs of White youths getting arrested for painting graffiti on the streets that the anti-white police force said violated the laws against hate. I saw farm trucks drive by and occupants throw Molotov cocktails from the beds at the apartments and tent camps of the third-worlders to show their disgust and disapproval of their replacement.

The night before I was to carry out the mission, I engaged in a personal objective that I knew was risky. During the early years of my marriage to Tiffany, I had worked in a wood fiber company some distance from the location where I was staged, but it was visible in the distance. It consisted of a lumber yard faced on one side by the old railroad bed, and a huge outdoor kiln that turned nonstop day and night as the workers filled the shaving boxes with pine and cedar logs. After exiting the kiln, the shaving material would be blown high into a huge container bin that extended hundreds of feet into the sky to await being dropped into the facility for bagging. On top of this huge holding container was a caged ladder that led to the entry shaft which consisted of an elbow that frequently clogged up. When it clogged, we would ascend the tremendous height to bang on the elbow in attempts to unstop the shaft. Many times while doing this I could survey the entire town of Silver springs. Directly above the shaft was the flag pole. To get onto the flagpole platform, you had to push a hinged door up from the bottom in order to gain access to the flag. At one time there was a chain and padlock on the hinged platform, but I never saw it locked. The first day we arrived to gather our intel, I could see in the distance that over the U.S. flag, was floating that damned Moloch star. Our people had become so incredibly brainwashed that they really believed that the Rothschild state of Israel deserved to be protected above our own interests.

I traveled in the dark down the railroad bed with only my bag on my shoulder. It took about an hour for me to walk the distance and I cautiously approached and watched as the night shift mongrel workers started filling the boxes with logs. The ladder access was not illuminated nor was it in direct sight of the work area, so I began to climb with confidence that no one had seen me. When I got to the top of the cage, I saw the rusted old padlock still laying on the platform. I pushed it open and stood under the disgraceful flags waving above me. There was a light shining on them but I was betting that at eleven o'clock at night, no one was watching the flag. I was a bit nervous because if I was caught, I would definitely be arrested and executed. I was hoping that this little flaunt of confidence would inspire our people, and after tomorrow, they would see real action in terms of resistance against the hostilities being perpetrated against them.

I took out my Confederate battle flag from my pack and removed the flags of oppression that I had equated with Babylon. As I raised the flag of my ancestors, that beautiful star studded cross, my heart swelled with pride. I heard trumpets sound inside my soul. I thanked God at that moment for allowing me to have the courage to do what I was doing.

I climbed under the platform and took the chain and applied my big padlock so that anyone who attempted to remove my flag would have to crawl back down and get bolt cutters. I then took out a couple sticks of cold weld, mixed them together and placed them so that the platform door could not be opened even after the chain was cut. I hoped whoever was assigned the task of removing my flag would get royally pissed at my handiwork.

As I descended the ladder, the hopper blower shut off. I knew what that meant. I stepped down onto the platform quietly as I heard voices below me. It was dark on the platform, and I had not been seen, but I was going to have to hide somewhere fast. I still had hundreds of feet to go before I was in the clear and I was sure that an employee was about to start toward me. There was a sledgehammer laying by the elbow that was left so that it wouldn't have to be brought up every time the elbow clogged. I grabbed the sledge and tossed it toward the empty side yard. When the Hispanic got to the platform I was on the other side of the hopper, watching with my knife in hand. He looked around briefly and yelled down at the others in Spanish and they seemed to laugh at him because he was going to be forced to climb back down to try and find another sledgehammer. When he was halfway down, I opened the bin door on the hopper and shoved the two flags in. That would cause a major disruption as they entered the factory below. It would take a considerable amount of work and resources to unstop the machines once the flags plugged the vent where shaving product was bagged.

As he neared the bottom, I started my descent with my heart racing the entire time. I no longer heard voices, so I was hoping that I was near success. When my feet hit the pavement, I heard the voices around the corner. I ran at breakneck speed through the unlit side yard and dove into the woods. The tracks lay just ahead, and I walked back to my location above the migrant housing center.

On the day that two migrant buses were to arrive with nearly one-hundred Burmese refugees, I was in position on a sloped power line that came to a point, much like a peninsula where an intersection crossed below.

I was facing the street with the least amount of traffic and, after my mission was accomplished, I would head up the peninsula into the woods and disappear. From that location I could navigate my way through a forest that I knew like the back of my hand. I knew every hole, cliff, drain and culvert from there to my grandfather's farm, which is where the transport team would pick me up. The designated spot was the bridge where Tiffany had been found.

As I watched through the scope awaiting the buses, I saw two men in the far distance on the caged ladder unable to get to the Southern banner I hoisted. I chuckled as they made multiple trips up and down only to be unsuccessful. My flag was still waving proudly when I spotted a Lexus pulling up to the office building adjacent to the tent camps and, to my surprise, the bastard stepped out and walked into the office. My heart was beating fast, and I held him in my crosshairs the entire time he was in view, but I refrained from killing him momentarily. As the buses came into view, I saw him reemerge from the office building with a few other office people with tablets and papers in hand as if to direct the proceedings of the initial relocation stage. I was tempted beyond measure. My job was to take out both bus drivers in an attempt to make anyone afraid of transporting migrants. I was well aware that I could damage my credibility as a leader by allowing myself to be overtaken by this temptation, but I was unable to stop it. Was it going to be any less damaging to their cause if I took out the President of the organization who was making it possible to invade our homes?

I was dialed in at 400 yards and I rested the hairs on his chest. He seemed to have a flirtatious moment with a woman beside him as I took a deep breath and squeezed. I did not bother to look at the scene at all. I knew when I pulled the trigger that he would be dead. I was staged at the edge of the woods and as soon as I pulled the trigger and was off and running with the rifle on my shoulder. I ran like a bolt of lightning to make as much time as possible. If I arrived early to the meet up spot, I had no problem killing time in the woods, but I did not want to have to try and throw off a pursuit. I heard the explosion at the police station but never slowed down. I was confident that I would hear all about it when I was taken to the Old School house to discuss why I deviated from the original plan.

As I traveled, my pace finally slowed. I stopped long enough to catch my breath and listen for any clues that I was being chased. I only heard sirens slightly in the distance. I guessed by the time and my speed that I had already run almost two miles. I couldn't help but think of my high school days running cross-country with Tiffany. Running was much harder in your thirties but easier when your life depends on it. When I reached the stone foundation of my great-great-grandfathers' house, I certainly knew where I was. I did not own the property where it sat anymore but the remaining portion of the farm that I lived on was less than five-hundred yards away. I remember when the house was still standing. It was sad for me to stand there and know what had befallen our people. I was not the only descendant of the rugged people who had lived on this site, but I was sure I was the only one trying to save our race from extinction.

I did in fact arrive early at the bridge and, out of curiosity, I wanted to see if my cabin was still there. I walked past my deer stand and stayed in the woods until I could barely see over the hill. My cabin was gone. The area where it stood had been leveled and my drive had become the entrance to a parking lot for heavy equipment. I figured it was a staging area for the mining company to begin stripping my land. I observed carefully before approaching but I had enough time to take my pocket screwdriver and remove the valve stems from everything with an inflatable tire. I cut the fuel lines and broke off spark plugs. I knew it was a minor setback for them, but it was satisfying for me.

I returned to the bridge and waited. Darkness was complete and I saw the headlights in the quiet distance. I was feeling a sense of relief. The van slowed just before the bridge and as I stepped out of the woods, the door slid open as it stopped barely long enough for me to get in. I sat on the bench seat and breathed deeply. Jason was riding shotgun. He was a builder and a good friend. As he handed me a thermos he wagged his head, "Zach Severs, you are one deadly son of a bitch, ain't ya?"

I didn't comment but I could not keep myself from grinning. Everyone was smiling and someone gave me a hardy pat on the back.

We returned to Fern Grove early the next morning and I was to report to the Old School at noon that day. I told Jessica what I had done, and she told me she would have done the same. There was never a moment when she questioned my actions. I was a little nervous about admitting what I had done but was content to accept the consequences. The meeting was less laid back than I thought, and I started to have concerns that I might be disciplined in some way. I sat alone at one end of the table as Jackson and Matt, along with a panel of FGIA members, looked at the information they gathered from the transport team and the media. A monitor was wheeled into the room and while I waited for the meeting to begin, I saw the media outlet's official story. I had indeed killed Anthony Vane, the man who stole the wife of my youth. I sat with my shoulders back and could have died a happy man regardless of how the FGIA viewed my actions. At precisely twelve o'clock, the monitor was shut off and Jackson spoke.

"Zachary Wayne Severs, you have chosen to implement your own judgement in the mission conducted on the night previous and have been brought here today to answer for your actions.

Deviation from direct plans and targets is strictly prohibited, and all of us here are sure you are aware of that, is that correct?"

"Yes sir."

"Is there anything you'd like to say to the panel in your own defense?"

I did want to say a few things but was hesitant. I hesitated and looked at the floor long enough for Jackson to bring me back with, "Zachary...do you have anything to say?"

"Before Mr. Vane appeared, I had every intention of carrying out the mission as planned... uh, when I was faced with the opportunity to remove him from his position, I will admit that I struggled with the choice. Before I pulled the trigger, I considered the Oath. In my heart I felt the better choice was to remove a coordinator of the war against us than simple foot soldiers. Given the opportunity to carry out similar missions I would be glad to redeem myself."

There was silence in the room for a few minutes. Then Matt spoke.

"We will review the case and look at the bylaws we have established. Return tomorrow at this time and we will finish the hearing."

"Yes sir."

"One other thing" Jackson said. "I caught a news blip that said a local factory near your staging area experienced an incident with a Confederate flag. You know anything about that?"

"No Sir." I figured I was in enough trouble as it was.

"The local resistance has been pretty active in the area. Probably some kids"

"Uh huh." Jackson said in a sarcastic tone of disbelief

I turned and dismissed myself

The following day, I was prepared for us to pack our bags and be removed from Fern Grove. What happened instead was a formal ceremony decorating me for valor in the field of service for the Aryan people. I was praised once again as a hero in our community and the stories of my service reached beyond our little community.

My job as a builder was basically over. The influx of young families flocking to our community gave us many assets, and we had no shortage of capable, aspiring men who were desperate to leave the old world of degeneracy behind. We had carpenters, welders, plumbers, mechanics, military men, the list goes on. I was aiding in the vetting process and helping teach classes on marksmanship and instruction in the field. I was busy planning another raid on the U.N. troops in a migrant-over-run town near the Alabama border called Barlow. The people there were in desperate need of an outside force to counter the brutality that they were experiencing due to the boot of the 'peacekeeping' forces.

Our missions had become more elaborate and sophisticated that, at many times, I felt as though there were more capable men than myself under my command, and at times, although I would not confess it, I longed to just live a simple life with Jessica and our children. Providence had not allowed it, or maybe God had designed it all. In my deepest thoughts I pondered what was truly happening. I sensed that I was in some sort of a vacuum, unable to free myself from the forces around me. We were sucked into the life we were living by means we could not control. While we seemed to gain ground at Fern Grove, the world outside continued to implode. The more we struck the enemy, the harder they came back on us and the townspeople that we help, never seemed to get free from the hand of our oppressors. I wondered how long we could go on this way, but I continued to live according to the Oath.

During a recon mission to Barlow, which was my first, we were able to get pictures of the base of operations of what looked like FEMA trucks along with the blue helmet foreign army. We had a force of at least a thousand men willing to go on the mission, but smaller units kept errors to a minimum. After much consideration, it was decided that I would lead a small group to take out a criminal gang element that was harassing the people in the town. We would cut the communication and cell towers, then set up roadblocks or barricade the roads in, and leave one road open for retreat. We had determined through the agency where the most violent gangs were housed and to my surprise, some of them were living quite luxuriously.

My particular mission that day was a small portion of the greater attack that we had planned. We were going to what I considered a mansion house which was a hot bed of criminal activity. Islamist terrorists, who had been invited by the traitorous government, were running a sex-trafficking ring from that location, and hundreds of local Aryan girls had been stolen and sold overseas or brutally murdered. Our men were more than ready. Ahmed Shu Han was the name of the bastard who was our main target. We planned on killing everyone at the mansion that night, but Ahmed would receive his sentence, and I would carry it out.

Ten of us were sent. We had cover from the outside by a young man I had trained named Andy. There were supposed to be no more than eight men at the residence that night but, counting the five we had to dispose of around the perimeter, there were thirteen. Once the other eight were accounted for, we made our move. We were aware that inside were women of Asiatic and Middle Eastern descent and possibly some of our own women. Prior to engaging, we could see that Ahmed was in the middle of a sexual encounter with an Asian woman and we decided no better opportunity would present itself. We cut the power to the mansion from the box outside, but a basement generator turned the power back on in about three seconds. Of course, this raised alarm inside the house, so we immediately charged the windows, shooting out the glass and sending shards all over the place. One man opened the big door out front and was taken down by one of our boys, I could hear shrieks of a feminine nature throughout the upper levels as Middle Eastern men came to the balconies only to be met with bullets. Two of the women were shot. I put my trust in the ability of our boys to dispatch our enemies as they had planned. My focus was on Ahmed. He came armed to the door of his suite and started to bring up his mini 9mm, but he could see that he had no chance. He looked to his left down the hall where one of his men was being administered his execution. More screams and another shattering of glass, but I held my stare on him as I removed my face covering. He looked at me with eyes full of hate and disgust that he had allowed himself to be caught in such a vulnerable situation, and he had no idea that his actions had brought about the hate that would end his life that night. He put his weapon down. I shot both his knees. He lay squirming in his own blood as he made a pitiful attempt to crawl back into the bedroom. I took a knife from my boot and grabbed the hair on his head while he was on his stomach. I stepped on one of his hands, crushing his fingers under my boot. The Asian woman screamed from the bed as I knelt low near Ahmed's ear and recited the death sentence... "Ahmed Shu Han, you have been found guilty of multiple crimes against the Aryan race. You will no longer ravage our women or occupy the land of our fathers." He grimaced as he knew he was seconds from death. "Your race will become as ashes under the feet of the Righteous...may you now roast in hell for eternity you sick, worthless mongrel." I pushed the blade in slowly and he struggled and gasped. He tried helplessly with one hand to prevent the knife from pushing through his skin, but he had no strength and was unable to stop the justice being swiftly invoked. The woman screamed again. Once my three-inch blade was in to the hilt, I made a quick sweeping motion with the blade and Ahmed jerked and quivered as his life left him.

I stood to exit, and my men were ready to go. We bolted from the front door to signal success to Andy and to continue with the retreat as planned, but there was no return signal. The other men did not notice right away and as we were heading in the direction of our transport, I took a young man named Josh with me to check on Andy, and we would meet them at the checkpoint where we were going to pick him up. We tried to move stealthily to Andy's position which was one-hundred-fifty yards from the mansion that was already showing movement from the women inside who were franticly trying to communicate with anyone they could. As we came upon Andy, I could see the pool of blood around his head momentarily before we were fired upon. I took two rounds, and Josh also took one to his arm before gunning down a Hispanic looking male with face tattoos.

Although I wouldn't give back the feeling of satisfaction I got from killing Ahmed, in the end, our trip to Barlow proved disastrous. Not only had I been shot twice with 9mm rounds, but our retreat was also hampered greatly. We were stranded unable to move and were forced to wait for help. I drifted in and out of consciousness and hindered Josh from being able to save himself.

My face had also been captured on battery-powered cameras and soon my name was once again all over the Jewish MSM. We also lost men on the other missions that night and some of them were taken into captivity. No one at Fern Grove knew what the fallout of this debacle would entail, and we all waited for the hammer to come down. I was being treated for wounds to my torso and leg and was lucky to be alive. Jessica stayed at my side, and it was during my stay at the hospital that she informed me she was pregnant again. I was determined to make sure that I could provide safety for my family, but I was beginning to wonder if a major change might need to be made for us.

Still not able to walk on my own, I was moved to the lower level of our home a week later where I was able to spend some quality time with Jessica and the children, but it was not free from concern. Word from the outside was not good. Our community had been discovered to be the hub for "terrorist" activity. As proud as I had been of the FGIA, the number of resources available to our enemies knew no limits. Not much time or energy gets spent on destroying one's enemy until they become a viable threat. Evidently, we had reached this level of resistance because what would follow in the weeks to come was hard to fathom.

The FGIA had received intelligence we were going to be basically shut off from the outside world. We'd been able, by and large, to trade with surrounding communities and share goods and commodities. Some of which we imported and others we exported. Troops began mobilizing around our logistical routes and it became nearly impossible for anyone to leave unless they were ok with being arrested, interrogated and possibly murdered. We began experiencing aircraft overhead during the dark hours of night. Elijah had been away, some said as far as Iowa, and hope he would be able to return diminished as weeks drew on. Supplies and food became low, and everyone knew we were under siege. We sent teams to the forest to see if any feasible evacuation was possible. There were FEMA men stationed all over every possible avenue out of Fern Grove. A man by himself could escape but not hordes of people at once. Our situation was gloomy, and I could tell it was bothering Jessica. I shared her concern and let her know that if we had to escape, we would. We kept light travel bags handy but although we were no strangers to living on the run, we had never attempted it with an infant.

On the night of Sept 17, 2028, there was a huge explosion that woke us from sleep. The Old School had suffered a direct hit from a missile as military helicopters were flying overhead. I knew there were people inside who were working on efforts to thwart an attack on our community. Likely thirty or more of our closest friends were either working or sleeping in the building at the time of the blast. In rapid succession, other buildings were hit, many of which I had helped construct in the early days of our arrival. We lost many lives that night. When the bombing ended, before we could even assess the damage, a full-on military invasion ensued, complete with Jewish Bolshevik tactics of civilian demoralization. It was every man and woman for themselves. There was hand-to-hand fighting as men were desperately fending off the onslaught of olive-skinned, mongrel troops as they threatened to ravage every home. Tanks rolled in to support the takeover. I thought in my mind that this must be similar to what it felt like to be in the Alamo or worse, Berlin, as the Soviet Jews destroyed the will of the German people.

Behind our brick home was a vast expanse of forest. I was not able to move as well as I would have liked and much of the burden fell on Jessica. Lia helped carry a bag, Jessica carried a backpack and her AK and, at times, helped carry Ephraim who was walking well but not able to keep up with us. I helped swap out carrying our son along with my .308 and a waist pack with ammunition for us both. We met Eric and his young wife and child in the woods and later met up with Matthew and his wife and two children as well. This made us all feel somewhat better about our chances than if we had to survive completely alone.

We walked into the night with only a vague sense of direction and were confident that we were heading north and within an hour, we would reach a county road called Buzzard Ridge Rd. The leg wound I had began oozing blood again. I was pushing my body beyond its limits, and we were as ragged as we could be. All of us awakened in the middle of the night to horrors we never dreamed of. We were all in shock and out of breath. Jessica, however, was as beautiful as the first time I saw her. Her blonde hair was a wavy mess. She never gave up on her white nightgown and the camo coat she wore over it and, on this night, I was reminded of the night she came to my cabin to confess that she didn't have a wood stove. If I had died that night, I guess I would have to say that I was a blessed man to have had such a daring beautiful woman at my side.

We gathered around to talk briefly and get some plan of action. I was in terrible pain but trying to be a help and not a hindrance. We decided to find a spot where a few FEMA or U.N. patrol vehicles could be easily taken without much disturbance. Matthew and Eric were very capable of pulling this off without me. We stumbled onto an old logging road which made walking through the forest much easier for me. We walked 'til daylight and came to a secluded portion of Buzzard's Ridge Rd. where we kept ourselves from view as we observed the road and the traffic. Only two cars passed in an hour. We traveled parallel to the road in the direction the cars had traveled until we saw an armored truck moving slowly our way. We got ourselves down and out of sight until the truck turned around and slowly traveled back in the direction it came. We waited patiently. Eric went into the woods to get water as we observed a jeep do as the armored truck did, turning around in the same pull off spot. The next time it was the armored truck again, and then the jeep precisely in fifteen-minute intervals. When Eric arrived, we concluded that the jeep would be our best option and as it pulled in to turn around, Jessica and Matthew's wife Laura would step from the woods and draw the occupants out. The rest would be a walk in the park.

As the jeep turned into the pull off, Jessica and Laura stepped out of the woods…the doors on the jeeps opened immediately as two young Chinese soldiers began talking flirtatiously toward our wives. I was 20 yards from the jeep and as the two chinks approached our women, Matt and Eric stepped out behind them. They turned and put their hands up and spoke as if we were supposed to understand them. Jessica and Laura simultaneously cut their throats. They were easily manipulated. To hell with them. We didn't even bother dragging them off the road. We briefly searched their bodies for wallets or spend cards, but none were found. They were likely implanted with chips that enabled them to buy anywhere without cash or plastic. Jessica spit on her would be assaulter. Laura did the same in imitation as she admired the grit and fortitude my wife had always displayed. We loaded ourselves into the jeep, it was tight, but we had very little luggage, and we only had about seven minutes before we would be pursued.

Matthew drove. He drove swiftly but not out of control. He was familiar with the area and knew how to get far away by using gravel and dirt roads. We drove west for two hours on a tank of gas and knew that we were not going to get far in a military jeep. We pulled into a town Matt was familiar with and he explained that he had cousins who lived in the Ozarks, and we couldn't be more than three hours from there, but we were going to have to get different transportation.

"Let's just steal a migrant van" Jessica suggested.

We drove until we scoped out a target and observed how we might obtain a more comfortable ride and hopefully more gas. In a department store parking lot, a Transport Van pulled in and parked. Out stepped what looked like Africans from any number of third world shit-hole countries. Eric's wife Rochelle brought us to laughter with her concern that the van would likely smell like shit, and unfortunately, she was right.

We were on our way again after commandeering the van but still did not have enough gas to get us to the community where Matt's extended family lived. We took the cell phone from the driver and turned the location off, which enabled us to gather some intel on what might be happening around us. We then acquired a federal spending card which we used to get some food, toiletry items, air fresheners and a full tank of gas.

Matt and I agreed to continue to his cousin Derek's farm, and Matt was able to contact him and tell him some of what had transpired, and he was eager to meet us and help in any way. Apparently, the Jewish world order had accelerated their agenda when it came to keeping revolutionaries in check. Derek had evidently suffered from attacks as well, so it was such a relief to know that we had nearly escaped disaster again, but we all knew it was temporary. Jessica lay against me as we tried to entertain Ephraim during the ride. As we rode, we dozed and nodded off and on until we finally came to a stop. It was almost dark as we shook ourselves free from sleep and began to look around. Matt said, "We're here," in a relieved tone.

The landscape looked similar to a war zone. Piles of rubble that might have been a barn or outbuilding were still smoldering. Fences were in a complete state of disrepair, and they looked as if heavy machinery had gone straight through them and rutted up crop fields and pastureland. The house sat on an incline about fifty yards from where we parked our migrant van. It was a big farmhouse that looked like it had been passed down through the generations.

Derek greeted Matt with a manly embrace and the two smiled and laughed as we awaited introduction. I heard Derek tease Matt about his thinning hair line and Matt returned the tease with a comment about Dereks thickening waistline. We were informed about a lot of the public perception of the FGIA, and how Derek was in contact with some groups who had fled to Idaho trying to get away from the chaos. His cattle had been poisoned, fields had been burned, and his barn set on fire, all done by men in dark suits in the middle of the night. His wife of twenty-three years was in the final stages of her bout with cancer, and Derek was just trying to hold on so he could maintain some sort of peacefulness during her final days. All things considered, Derek was in a very depressing situation and having us all arrive at his door was quite uplifting for him.

Once inside, as we sat at a long table, Lia and Matt's oldest son Jeremiah played with the toddlers in the living room. Derek had some coffee stashed away for hard times and apparently, hard times had arrived. He said that in the last few days, very few commodities could be found.   All the local stores had been looted to the point of being bare. He had stocked up on several things, and had been doing so for quite a while, but he had been forced to begin using his supplies because it wasn't safe for him to be in town, and he wasn't comfortable leaving his wife, Lynne.

We sat for a long while and conversed into the night. We

discussed the scriptures and hashed out our theological beliefs about how the Jews had obtained world domination. Was it in the cards for us to ever be free from their oppression? We talked about the goals each of us had and what we would like to accomplish with the rest of our lives, however short they might be. Derek had shed lots of light on what we would be capable of doing with his help. He wanted to remain as peaceful as he could until Lynne was gone, but he had been attacked on all sides to the point of giving up. The local ZOG traitors had nearly destroyed his heritage by their terror attacks on his property. He only had one barn with about fifty bales of hay left to count as anything worth monetary value and he was sure that they would be coming for the barn anytime. He had planned after Lynne was gone, to take his Armalite into town and end his own life in a gun battle with the ZOG police force. He admitted that he had no more reason to live. We tried to encourage him and gave him some hope that together we might be able to show a significant amount of resistance without having thoughts of ending his life.

We were tired and dirty. Jessica and I were given an upstairs room with a shower. Lia and Ephraim slept in the adjacent room, and I watched her as she climbed from the shower with her towel around her. She was not yet showing, and her body was healthy and tone. The German war eagle peeking out from the top of the towel and her wet blonde hair was down to her shoulders. She was still the epitome of everything I found attractive. She saw that I was watching her and met my gaze with those eyes that captivated me. She brought one hand up and uncinched the towel. It hung only briefly to her breasts before falling to the hardwood floor. As she stepped toward the bed, I sat up to meet her and her chest was level with my face. I put my arms around her and kissed her ever so gently as she ran her fingers through my hair. Our devotion to each other could not even be put into words. We made love.

Later she asked quietly, "Do you think we could make it to Idaho?"

I thought for a moment and tried to answer honestly. "The journey of a thousand miles begins with one step....do you want to go to Idaho?" I asked.

She thought and then answered, "I want to be far away from the chaos. I want to bare our children in peace."

We agreed to talk to the others and then ultimately make the decision that best fits our family.

At breakfast the next morning, I asked Derek about the Idaho option. He explained that the families who had left Northeast Arkansas for a new life in Idaho, had done so at the recommendation of a man named Elijah McLeroy. He was an old man who coughed a lot but was very knowledgeable and had contacts all over the former U.S.

We all looked at each other in disbelief and shock.

"Is Elijah still alive?" I asked.

"If he is, he's in Idaho... He said he had been cut off from his people in Tennessee and was facing arrest and execution if he was caught."

"We are those people." Matt said sorrowfully.

"Elijah created the intelligence agency that conducted most of the resistance missions in central Tennessee. We carried them out... with help of course... but we were uncovered as a hub for terrorist activity, and they came down like the Red Army on Berlin. We didn't stand a chance... that's what brought us here."

As we talked, our wives listened intently as Derek talked about wide open spaces and freedom from the chaos in the condensed, multicultural hell that our homeland had become. I thought briefly of Silver Springs and the land my grandfather had given me. I had buried it from my thoughts and was determined to never long for it again, but I could not help but wonder if they were following through with the mining operation. I wasn't certain that I wanted to know.

A week passed. We rested. Our children played. We bonded. We prayed. We sang together and ate together. We cared for Lynne and after two weeks, we dug her grave.

We left Derek alone with her on the hillside grave plot and we returned to the house. We were somewhat restless but at the same time reluctant to begin another journey of hardship. There was a desire among us to stay in the farmhouse and conduct our own raids on the town. We could live there somewhat comfortably and have room for our families to grow and build, but Derek reminded us of how quickly all of that could change. The number of resources being used against the people there, was vast. It was looking as though the U.N., with the help of FEMA, was conducting an extermination of Whites, and he was sure that they would not be done until the farm was in shambles and the house burned.

I lay awake that night in bed as Jessica lay beside me. She had a habit of falling asleep on my chest. As I drifted, I heard the hardwood floor creak on the downstairs level. I did not think much about it since the house was full and nearly every room occupied. I only became concerned when I heard voices outside. Jessica awoke as I grabbed my pants and covered my lips with my finger to keep her from startling the children. I moved slowly to the side of the window so as not to show my presence, and below I caught a glimpse of a hooded negro moments before a shotgun blast hurled him onto his back.

"Take that, you sumbitch." I heard Derek scream as I reached for my rifle. Jessica grabbed her AK and took the children into the closet. I quickly heard another blast and then heard the steps of Matthew and Eric as they came from their rooms, we reached the stairs and descended into the living room. It was dark and I called calmly for Derek to tell us where he was. He was staring out the bay window in the kitchen that had been blasted out as the moonlight revealed the bodies in the yard and moving dark figures out at the barn. They had just set fire to the hay in the last remaining structure on the farm. Without asking I raised my rifle.

"Don't bother..." Derek commanded. "...It's all over now."

I wasn't able to get a clear shot anyway. The men were retreating and had vehicles supplied to them which they couldn't acquire, build or even maintain on their own. It had always been clear to me that our destruction was orchestrated by those who had the money to empower the dark races to make war against us. Our enemy has known for centuries that they could not defeat us in combat on their own. They used money and influence to gain every powerful position in our land, the land that our ancestors settled and developed for us. This was a war by proxy and what I had come to realize is that almost all wars in our violent past have been the same. The enemy that stands to gain from the violence has always been the international Jew. Throughout the world wars, White men went toe to toe in a full-scale slaughter of each other as the Jewish bankers became rich. This trend continued unabated through the 20th century and into the 21st. Now, what is left of the dying White race is forced to contend with the flood of a third world invasion, brought to us by none other than the same enemy.

I was weary of only being able to kill these foreign invaders. It was much like being in the colosseum, being forced to fight a lion when Nero was the one who needed killing. Our people have no choice but to fight the lion, because the ones responsible for putting him in the arena will never present themselves on the battlefield.

As the fire raged out of control, we stood and watched from the house. The flames lit up the night. I could see tears of anger and rage welled up in Derek's eyes in the orange light.

All at once we heard a deep low grumble that sounded like distant thunder, but then the ground vibrated. The panes in the farmhouse rattled slightly and as we looked at each other, Matt said softly, "Earthquake."

After a few moments, another tremor occurred. It was about 2:00 in the morning. We knelt and prayed in the yard as the fire raged. I remember asking God for guidance and I remember Jessica holding my hand tightly on one side and Lia on the other. Matt's son Jeremiah held Lia's other hand.

Chapter 4

Setback

Idaho it was. We all decided that we wanted to get far away and find peace if we could. If it could be found in the wide-open spaces of the west, then we were determined to go there. I had agreed to accompany Derek into town to see if any provisions could be purchased or even traded for in the small rural Arkansas town. Unbeknownst to me was the fact that my picture was everywhere, and I began to get extremely paranoid. Evidently, I was wanted by the FBI and was suspected of being in the area. I had no idea that I had become so well known in the outside world. While inside a department store, I was looking through the clutter of cardboard and plastic wrap for anything of value but was not finding much. Derek was getting the last remnants of anything edible, which consisted of tomato juice and some lemonade drink mix, when I noticed a stock worker with purple hair say something quietly to another coworker, whose eyes then glanced at me. At that moment I knew I needed to go. I whispered to Derek that I would see him at the farmhouse later as I brushed past him in the aisle and darted through the double doors to the stockroom, and then out the back exit. There was a short black-haired woman smoking a cigarette at a break table who saw me swiftly use the dumpster to scale the board fence. I looked back through the cracks and saw three police cars pulling into the lot. Deputies ran to cover the exit that I had just escaped from, and the others entered the front with guns drawn.

I was not one hundred percent healed from my wounds, but I was healthy enough to make a good run. I did not want to lead the authorities back to the farm and, to be honest, it was at that point that I was unsure of what to do. I was caught off guard for the first time in my life and I nearly froze. I kept running and had no knowledge of the area or landscape. I had done a lot of running over the last few years, but I had always had a destination, and I always knew my surroundings. I had left my pistol in Derek's truck and at first, I felt this was a terrible mistake, but later it proved the one thing that may have saved my life.

I tired quickly. I turned around on a bluff to see if anyone was following me and I was in fact being pursued. This was a time unlike any other for me. I had never been in such a predicament. I ran on ahead and instead of running out of town, I ran into the back of a grocery store on a street parallel to the department store. I began to hear sirens on the street just about two blocks away and so I jumped into the concrete drainage ditch and followed it through the wooded lots behind a large shopping mall. I was really stuck. I thought of possibly stealing a car or trying to reach a high area so that I could see my surroundings, maybe I could possibly blend in somehow. Then I heard the dogs.

I liked hounds. I had always loved their natural ability to track prey and use their noses to pick up trails that were days old. On this day, my appreciation of them turned to disgust. I felt a little bit of panic and tried to remain calm by taking deep breaths. I drug my feet in the water as much as possible before exiting the drainage ditch. At the edge of the woods, I saw police cars pulling into the strip mall parking lot so I ducked back into the ditch and headed back in the opposite direction toward Derek's truck. I heard the dogs and their trainers pass up beside me at about sixty yards away and I descended the slope when I heard the bustle of leaves coming behind me. An athletic young negro deputy was right on my heels. He must have come from the cars that pulled into the strip mall because no one else was even that close. I knew I was not going to outrun him, so I turned to stand my ground. If I had my gun in my possession at that time, I would have just shot him but would have alerted the whole town with my gunfire. He plowed into me before I could even think. He literally knocked the wind out of me and broke one or more of my ribs. He cuffed me and before the other officers got there, he got in a few cheap shots to my gut that hurt like hell. He called me some names, like "White honkey trash, racist piece of shit", nothing too outlandish or deeply thought. He then lied and said I assaulted him, which was fair because I would have killed him if I could, and I still would have if it were possible.

I had succumbed to my worst fears. All I dreaded had become reality. In their minds I was a murdering psychopath and if their brand of justice was to be served, I would be executed. I thought of Jessica and the children as they put me face down in the back of the cruiser. My hands were burning from the tightness of the cuffs and my ribs hurting when I breathed. I was getting childish jeers from the officers who were quite proud of themselves. Some of them were saying things about how I killed my wife, and some said I was a cult leader. All of it sounded so ludicrous.

I was transported to a holding facility there in Arkansas where I was held on charges that were a mile long, ranging from defacing government property, to murder, and even treason. The FBI was going to conduct their interrogation of me that evening, but I wasn't in the mood. They asked me first about Derek and if I knew him. I could only hope at that point that he had made it back and somehow had gotten everyone away from the farmhouse. If the cops already had Derek and were interrogating him, they wouldn't tell me. They would let me tell them a string of lies when they already knew the truth because they are sneaky lying scumbags. I simply sat silent and then one of the head interrogators tried to show everyone

90

how tough he was and tried to bully me and threaten me by telling me he would find out anyway and then I would be sorry. I told him he had a feminine voice and looked like a homosexual. I received his fist for that one, but the thought of being able to bring him to that level of anger brought me great pleasure. I felt blood trickle into my beard from my lip. I was determined to piss them off even if it meant my death.

"We know your gang is planning another strike. Tell us where, and all this can be over." These asshats are always so predictable and stupid, and their tactics are nothing but worn-out drivel.

"Are all ZOG-bots faggots, or just you? I mean, how many times a week do...?" My question was cut short because he hit me with a roundhouse punch that got me pretty good. My nose began to bleed and with my hands restrained behind my back I could not stop the flow. It finally clotted but not before I looked like a bloody mess. They halted their questions.

It seemed like they were trying to wear me down. The agents sat there silently for hours blowing cigarette smoke and taunting me. They would say things about Jessica or Lia and even Tiffany, just to see if they could make me angry enough to tell them something or anything. The things they said were to each other for my benefit, knowing I had no choice but to overhear their conversations which they kept low to purposely make me try to hear. They were so ignorant about my life that nothing they said scared me at all. My body language and taunting eventually ended with them losing their patience with me. I beat them at their own game until the game started to be who could hit me and knock me unconscious. The third agent must have done the trick because I don't remember anything after that.

I was unaware of the passage of time, nor did I know if I was even in the same building or state. I woke in a cell face down on the concrete floor. My lip felt fat and tender, and a couple of my teeth felt loose. My ribs still hurt when I breathed, and I had a raging headache. Hours went by in solitude and finally the flap on the door opened and a deputy dropped in an envelope. Inside contained my charges and court dates for those charges. I was going to be sent back to Kentucky to stand trial for Tiffany's murder, and Delwin's murder as well. I was also formally charged with the murder of Ahmed, which had been captured on video. At the present moment though, I was curious if they were unaware of the fourteen people I had dispatched of over the last four years or if they had figured out, I had killed Dr. Vane. I knew they were going to use me as an example, but they didn't have a fraction of the so-called crimes I had committed. I thought of how my dreams of living in peace and raising a family were not going to happen. I sat in silence for days.

Jessica sat alone crying. I saw her through the window of the farmhouse when the fire started. I saw her trying to get Ephraim out of his bed and pick up her AK. Lia was screaming and I was trying to calm them, but no one could hear me. I finally yelled out in desperation in order to be heard.

I awoke alone in my cell in a cold sweat, breathing heavily and staring at the wall. I had awakened myself as I yelled out in my sleep. Being away from my family was driving me insane. I felt as though I would do anything to get back to them, but I knew that no matter what I did or said, they were going to sentence me to death, and I knew I was already as good as dead.

After what seemed like a month, I was taken to Silver Springs and housed in the regional facility about sixteen miles from the Justice Building where I would see a judge.

The morning of my court appearance, I was given ten minutes to shower. I was led down the hallway where officers had pulled into the Sallyport, and I would be loaded into the van. When the door buzzed and I stepped through to approach the two officers in charge of transporting me, I could barely contain myself. I did everything in my power not to smile, or even look at Matt as he said to the other officers loud enough for me to hear, "This the killer they've been trying to catch for so long?"

The deputy behind the counter replied, "Yeah. He's a real piece a'shit if he did what they say. You two guys work Fed transport very long?"

Eric was clean-cut and dressed the part as well as Matt. They looked very strong and sharp and conversed with the county deputies so well that I thought I might be hallucinating.

"I've been with the agency for about eight years, but I just got moved to this area. Sounds like you guys are experiencing a lot of resistance fighting from what we've been told."

I just kept my head down and then Matt commanded me to put my knees in the chair provided, as he placed shackles on my ankles.

"Hands behind your back." He said.

Matt put the cuffs on, and I was ready to go. The officers at the regional facility never suspected a thing. We had to go through two doors to get to the transport van and we all played our parts until the sun came through as the control room operator opened the Sallyport door. I was in the back separated from my friends and we were not able to talk through the glass. All I knew was that I wasn't going to court, and I was nearly in tears of joy as we neared the highway.

I rode in the back of the van for about forty-five-minutes and then Matt pulled off the highway onto a gravel road that eventually became a dirt road. I was only able to see out the front glass as we pulled into a secluded area. I saw a late 90's model Chevrolet parked in a shady spot that looked like an overgrown parking area at an old quarry. We stopped and I saw Jessica get out of the passenger side of the truck with both hands over her mouth and tears in her eyes. She looked intently at the van as though her hope could not be satisfied fast enough. When Matt opened the door for me, he immediately went to work on my cuffs and shackles. He had to do so while contending with the woman whose arms were wrapped around me, running her fingers through my hair as we kissed franticly. I was finally free to give her a full embrace when Eric said, "Y'all can have the back seat of the truck, but we gotta get going."

I was weak but I picked her up like a groom carrying his bride and made my way to the truck with her. Matt and Eric ran the van over a cliff into a manmade lake below, hiding any evidence of our location. They climbed into the truck with us. Eric manned the CD player. In a moment of triumph, we pulled out onto the highway as SKIDS blasted 'Alternative Ulster.' I had so many questions as to how they were able to pull it off and I had lots to tell them about my awful experience, but I was too busy enjoying Jessica's tongue as she was making up for lost time. We had to calm down for Matt and Eric's sake.

"Guys!" Matt said, "We will get a hotel in about four hours, if you can wait that long."

We smiled at each other with our noses still pressed together.

Chapter 5

Onward

Derek had been detained for a few hours the day I was arrested, but nothing could be found connecting him to me. They took his guns and gave him court dates to appear but eventually let him go. He said that had it not been for the need to return and tell what happened, he would have just had a shootout there at the department store. Eric and Matt went to work immediately on a plan to get me out and they accomplished it masterfully. The bodies of the agents who were supposed to pick me up for my court appearance had likely already been found but it would take a while to figure out their identities since they were not locals. The FGIA had contacts within the system and Matt was able to make contact with them and pinpoint when my court appearance was scheduled. They had spent lots of time away from Laura and Rochelle and their children, while gathering intel and stalking agents so they could pull off my escape. I was indebted to them, but they assured me that they were honored to call me a friend and brother. They knew I would do the same for them.

As I recounted some of my trials to them, I think it was a general consensus among us that we needed to get on with our plans and start for Idaho.

They brought me a change of clean clothes and a pistol. I even got a new pair of boots courtesy of some dead federal soy boys. I was feeling human again. We stopped at a hotel and paid for our rooms with some prepay cards. Jessica and I got a room together next to Matt and Eric. The next morning, they accused us of keeping everyone awake on the whole second floor.

The rest of our families were at a farm in western Missouri. Derek was able through his contacts to form what could be likened to an underground travel system. White families throughout the Ozarks and beyond were helping refugee families like us get relocated. All of our children were safe as far as we knew, and there were resources and manpower amidst the collapse of the system. While there were many Whites still under the spell of decades of brainwashing, there were many who were breaking away. It seemed like everywhere we went; Whites were having children in larger numbers. My generation, before society began to really implode, was subjected to huge amounts of conditioning. Every movie, every music video, all the books, billboards, and advertisements were nothing but race mixing propaganda. The generation before me was convinced by those in the economic world that only having one or two children was now our moral obligation since the world was becoming so populated. Unfortunately, the propaganda worked on many Whites, and we saw the emergence of a generation of mixed-race mongrels. All the while, our borders were wide open and the dark races continued to have large families who relied on the help of Whites to feed them, clothe them, and put roofs over their heads. The good people in America were convinced that the world would continue as always even if the demographics changed, and in a single generation the world's population of Whites dropped from 15% to about 8%. During the years of the viruses, I had suspected that the creators who patented the diseases had used genetic markers to target the Aryan race and many whites who put their faith in the medical system died within a few years. With the all-out extermination being conducted against us, I assumed that our population numbers were lower now.

We journeyed out of Missouri and stopped near the Spring River in the northeastern tip of Oklahoma. We were all happy to be back together and excited about our future. I began to see Jessica's body start to show signs that she was carrying another child. Eric and Rochelle were expecting again as well. Derek stayed with us and helped navigate our path and also made himself useful in other ways. He became an uncle to the children in many respects. It seemed to fit him, being that he and Lynne were unable to have children. He fished with them, talked with them, and kept them occupied while we conducted the basic living activities needed when traveling in a quasi-caravan like we were.

We still had the Chevrolet, complete with a topper now. We had a Jeep Cherokee that Matt, Laura, and their children occupied. Eric and his growing family had a faded red Durango with a white door and green hood. None of the vehicles we had were in prime condition, but they were enough to get us moving in the direction we wanted to go. We spent a few weeks at a salvage yard just scraping together the Jeep and Durango to make our journey somewhat more comfortable.

We drove on into Nebraska. We took our time, stopping at the houses along the suggested routes, sometimes working for provisions and food. Sometimes families would ask for us to check on their kin when we reached Idaho. Many of those who helped us were people who could have been easily convinced to go with us, and some tried to convince us to stay with them.

When we reached the small town of Cedar Bluff on the North Platte River, in the far west of Nebraska, we came in contact with Robert and Maggie Yasser. It was here in Cedar Bluff, with the help of these generous saints of God that we really got on our feet again. We needed stability for when the new children were born, and we needed to take a break from the traveling lifestyle. We were worn out from living that way and when I looked in the mirror, I could see that I was aging.

It had been almost 5 months since I was rescued at Silver Springs and much had transpired in the world of Babylon while we were traveling and living our lives apart from that hell. A disease had developed among the negro population due to a genetic propensity and those in America were dying at unprecedented rates, much higher than in their native Africa. It was said to be a wasting disease that left the body in a zombified state before death was final. Some people were saying that entire portions of the eastern former U.S. was uninhabitable due to the stench of rotting corpses. It was almost as if Divine intervention had interrupted the slaughter and rape of God's people. There were still roving Mexican drug gangs operating within our borders, or what used to be the American border but from what we could tell, they operated further south.

We had been at Bob and Maggie's only a few weeks when the Great Quake was felt. The tremors that shook Derek's farmhouse were just the initial shock before the New Madrid fault line gave way. We suffered minor damage, but the main quake was powerful enough to wake us all as the windows rattled in our rooms. The towns along the Mississippi River were, by and large, swept away by redirected water ways. Many of the NGO headquarters were destroyed in that area and untold thousands of alien invaders had been swept to their deaths. We continued to pray for guidance and ask our Father for wisdom, courage and strength as the world changed around us.

Bob was a teacher of theology and had pastored a church

there in Cedar Bluff and led the entire congregation from a Judeo-brainwashed sect to an understanding of the actual identity of who true Israel is. We sat at his feet on many nights as he told the story of how what was transpiring in the world could be traced to the struggle between Jacob and Esau. What we all had felt in our hearts was true, Bob was able to show us in the scripture as a fact. The scriptures that had always alerted me about the Jews being anti-Christ and that they were of the synagogue of Satan, were brought out and examined under the story of Esau's hatred for his brother and the subsequent prophecy's pertaining to their descendants. Bob explained the Old Testament prophecies to us from Obadiah, Isaiah, and Ezekiel in ways that I had not been able to understand before. It became clear to us all that modern Jews were never God's chosen people and that true Israelite's were found among the White race. According to the prophecies of Obadiah, Esau assisted the Babylonians in the destruction of Jerusalem and for this, he had been marked by God and would be wiped from the face of the earth at some future point by the hand of Jacob. There had been a prophesied time when Esau would have control over the earth, and due to the creation of the monetary system, he was able to do so. It had transpired over the course of several generations of debauchery, sin, and hedonistic behavior that allowed this to happen. It will end when Christ returns again to make the salvation promised to us complete. As of now, we only see in part what will become a reality.

This gave us all tremendous hope. We had been at some of our lowest and most desperate times before our connecting with Bob and Maggie. Our own walk with God which each of us had pursued alone, was shared but never thought of as a collective salvation. Bob reminded us of Matthew 1:21, "He came to save *His* people, from *their* sin." We all realized that we were His before He ever saved us, and from that time forward, we did our best to act like we were, His.

As a young Christian, I never had a desire to pursue unity with the other races even when I incorrectly assumed that they could be my "spiritual brethren". 1 John 3:14 says, "This is how we know that we have passed from death unto life, because we love the brethren."

I believe our desire to have unity with our true White brothers and sisters around the world is the only way to fulfill the meaning of brotherly love. I knew then as now that our people all over Europe, South Africa, and Australia were fighting for our race every bit as much as we were, and I prayed for them.

I remembered when I first learned how the civilians in Dresden were burned alive in the manmade hell storm, that I felt sick inside. Even though I may not have personally been responsible for the actions, I still felt the need to pray for the collective forgiveness for raising our hand against our brothers in Germany. The scripture in Revelation 18:24 was true in that the whore of Babylon was found with the blood of all slain upon the earth. Even the blood that I had personally spilt with my own hands was like that spilt by David. It was thrust upon me by my enemies who forced my hand. The very same enemies who surrounded David surrounded us.

Just prior to Owen being born, many towns in the west experienced bombings similar to what we experienced at Fern Grove on that fateful night. It seemed to be rather uncoordinated. As bad as it was, there were several missed targets and some of their aircraft even crashed into the desolate areas of vast wilderness. Our men were able to shoot drones from the sky and I was able to do so as well. I was in a barn loft watching some of these events take place while Jessica gave birth to our son Owen in a bomb shelter nearly two miles from where I was. There was not enough room in the shelter for anyone except the women assisting with the birth. The men kept a watchful eye on the surroundings. I heard many explosions throughout a week's time but only one was close enough to cause concern. With Bob as our guide, we traveled to a nearby town which had suffered a direct hit, to see the devastation, provide some relief, and bury the dead.

While there, we helped pull bodies from the rubble of a school building where citizens had gathered to pray, according to survivors. I was standing beside an exterior concrete wall in what was the inside of a classroom. Among the debris were many bodies, and as we removed several, I came across a young blonde girl whose body was mangled and bloody. Her features were pretty but blue and lifeless. I held her for a few moments in my arms and everyone paused in sheer agony that our little ones had to suffer. I trusted that she was with her Creator now and the trial of this life was over for her. As bad as death is, life for some is worse. I tried to take solace in that.

Moments after that, I heard a cry. I had just handed the girl off to another crew as we sort of worked like an assembly line. It came from behind two fallen filing cabinets that were supporting a portion of sheet rock and 2x4 wall. Clutter and building materials had to be removed but I was able to reach the little voice with my hands as I lay on my stomach. She came to me, very afraid and crying. She looked identical to the little girl I just handed away to the burial crew. I heard a local man say, "That's Della Rogers!"

She was the twin sister of Stella, the deceased little girl I had just held, and now she was hanging onto me for dear life. She could not have been more than five years old and her entire household was killed that night. No one protested when we returned to Cedar Bluff with her in tow. She adapted quickly and played with all the children among us, which totaled seven after Eric and Rochelle had their daughter. Owen was only a month old when Jessica helped assist in the birth of the baby girl who they named Guinevere Rose.

The women organized meetings for the children that could have been called 'school', but they never allowed their schedule to override what the children needed from day to day. They just usually always did it together. Some days they just explored the world around them. Other days they would learn a small bushcraft skill and learn about animal care. The children loved the gardening projects and watching the seeds they planted sprout up. I watched Jessica during that time as she seemed to relish the life she had found. The transformation she made was quite a testimony in lieu of the life she had before we met in Silver Springs. In fact, it was hard to think of life in any less way than what we had chosen to live. So many of our people rode a train of temporary comfort and it cost them their lives. Not necessarily literally, although in some cases it was true, but those who never acted in any way to help secure a future for our race never lived in my opinion.

The men and I continued to help in the community, and we even traveled into the countryside to visit a crash site of one of the bomber planes. Matt had mentioned the possibility that the pilots may have ejected before the crash. If that were true, then we could have an enemy among us and we were not willing to take chances. There was no mistaking who was responsible for the attacks. That demonic star of Remphan still visible in the wreckage did not surprise any of us. There was no sign of a body or bodies, but there was no chance anyone would have survived if they had been aboard the plane at the point of impact.

We stayed at distances as we walked so that we might be able to see any signs of human activity. We crossed a tributary creek of the Platte, and high in an overhanging cliff, Eric spotted a fire pit.

It may have been just locals camping but we made note of it. Downstream was what appeared to be hay-bale wrapping hanging partially in low branches above the creek. Some of the material was floating in the water but hung up on the branches. From a distance, we all knew what it could be and sure enough, it was a parachute.

We were about six miles from Bob's farm and bunkhouses where we were staying. It was agreed among us that when we returned, we would set up a night watch so that we would not be taken off guard. It was only a few days after that, a White family in a neighboring town, who were active in weapon repair and reloading, was subjected to an attack on their home. In fact, the husband was beaten severely while his wife was raped and murdered. One of their children escaped but the man is not expected to live. This was a prominent family in the area who others respected and liked. This was a family Bob had known his entire life. Similar occurrences happened again in different places. Finally, one survivor was able to give a description of the men and one of them was killed during a home attack. He was Hispanic but according to the report given, not all the men were of that nationality. At the least, one of them was taller and had military fatigues. It appeared that with the negro arm of their assault waning, the kikes were having to take a physical part in their attempts to genocide us.

Matt, Eric, and I were in agreement that we could try to oust this pestiferous, little enemy that had raised its head. We discussed ways in which we might track them, look for their habits, and study their targets to see what they had in common. There was no doubt that those who were being targeted were shining lights in their communities. It occurred to us all that Bob could very well be on their hit list. Someone with intel was planning these attacks and so anyone who had been outspoken, or done any activism on behalf of White Christian societies was subject to terrorism. Evidently, our enemy had resorted to guerrilla tactics in a new ground war against our people. We stayed on high alert and focused on our eventual departure which we had somewhat lost sight of, due to the kindness of our hosts, but Idaho was our goal.

I was on night watch when they came. From the loft of the barn, I could see them approaching. They never suspected me, and I was able to eliminate two and wound another. There were five men that I could see. As the lead man approached the back door of the house, I sent his brain matter into the yard not much different than if I had shot a pumpkin. The others, confused as to whether they should run, or duck for cover, scrambled. Without knowing my position, they were unable to remove themselves from my sights. As one of them hunkered down beside Bob's truck on the side facing me, the lights in the house came on. I squeezed the round off just as the figure began to rise in flight. Instead of a kill shot, he lay bleeding out, with a gaping hole in his left lung. As the others ran, I fired a shot towards the center of a moving target but was not confident that I was successful.

The lights at the bunkhouse came on as well and everyone waited until I gave the all-clear before stepping outside to see what had transpired. Everyone had a weapon. Jessica in her white gown and her AK in hand, Jeremiah had an Armalite and Lia stood beside him in her nightgown. I was conscious of what was going on between them even though it felt like I could not give it my full attention. The thought of Lia having feelings for the boy was more of a reminder that I was getting older, not that I was against the inevitable facts of nature. Lia looked like her mother and in all reality, not too much different than Jessica. Matthew and Laura had raised a good son thus far, and I saw no other prospects around for Lia and didn't really want any. If they eventually started a family, I wouldn't protest.

I approached the dying man beside Bob's truck and shined a light into his face. Bob met me there with his rifle in hand as Maggie stayed by the door, watching her husband carefully. He frothed bloody bubbles from his mouth and was about to expire when I told him to 'burn in hell.' His eyes moved in the direction of the light, and I knew he comprehended what I had said. His expression of hate faded. As the women examined the bodies and pilfered their pockets for information, I took Matt and Eric to the spot near the edge of the yard where I fired on the third man. This presented a dangerous situation and if I had it to do over, I would not have fired the third time. We found a significant amount of blood, but no body. The small tree lined gulley that separated the yard from the pastureland was dark and would provide enough cover for a wounded man to hide and also be dangerous. The pasture was about twenty fenced acres before the wooded area beyond could be reached. There were about two hours before daylight and I felt like we were at a disadvantage by going after a wounded man who, if properly concealed, could potentially kill any of us. We agreed to return after daylight, so we went back to our families.

Back at the house, Laura and Rochelle had helped Bob and Derek dispose of the bodies while Jessica helped Maggie prepare a large breakfast. It was an early morning for us all. As we ate together, it was time to discuss with Bob our plans to move further west. I knew that Bob was willing to let us stay and may have been hurt that we intended to move on, but I spoke to him about growth and the opportunity for him to share and help other White families as they looked to do what we had done. His sadness gave way to happiness when he considered the growth and the hope that our race was still resilient enough to live on in a world hellbent on destroying them. He was thankful for the time we spent there, and we assured him that what we had gained by being his guests was priceless. He

105

knew of a few like-minded families who had gone to Idaho before the quake and through an archaic but effective mode of letter writing, similar to the pony express, they kept in contact with their kin who remained there in Nebraska in order to keep the connections needed for growing White communities all over the western states if possible. A family member wrote down directions to a community willing to give us a start due largely to the fame we had attained in the underground world of White pride. My exploits had given me a status that I was oblivious to. He gave us a word to use as a pass code when we arrived. Strangely, the password was, 'Elijah.'

During the course of the two years, we lived well in Cedar Bluff. I stayed close to Bob and learned from him the fine theological aspects of the scriptures, coupled with the forgotten ancient history of our people. One thing that I was astounded by, was the man's ability to remember the dates and peoples throughout history which seemed to be so pertinent to our time, as though every step our ancestors had taken had been the fulfillment of biblical prophecy, and we were standing as a righteous remnant of God's people, who God Himself promised He would have at the end of the age. I became obsessed with the flight of the tribe of Ephraim into Europe after the fall of the Assyrian Empire to Mido-Persians. According to secular history and all the Jewish textbooks, all that had ever been taught to us about the origin of our own people, was that they appeared in the Caucus Mountain region around 600 BC. This was ironically the same time that the oppressors of the Ten Northern tribes of ancient Israel in Assyria were destroyed. Moreover, even the Jewish historian Josephus told in his writings that the lost tribes were beyond the Caspian Sea and were in great multitudes. After learning these things, I felt as though our race has a special place in the eyes of God. No wonder God had blessed the White nations above all others in the world. No wonder those outside of it wanted to destroy it out of pure jealousy and hatred. No wonder the lesser people of the third world want what they are unable to produce for themselves. Aryan people had created the most harmonious, peaceful, and desirable societies on the planet while trusting and living in obedience to their Creator, but as generations fell to the seductions of the enemy, those blessings began to wane. The punishment that we were suffering was not necessarily God's punishment, although in some cases that may well be true, but it was more due to the fact that God knows what happens when His people invite strangers into their lands and try to live with them in a single society. Those dangers were not stopped by God, because He wrote in the scriptures why we were to avoid these situations and what would happen if we didn't. If a person decides that this equals punishment from God, then I wouldn't argue that view. I was willing to accept it, and strive to correct my paths, to get back to the blessings we had in generations past.

We finished breakfast after the sun came up and since I had been up all night, Matt and Eric convinced me to stay and be an armed presence there at the farm while they investigated the blood trail. Derek went with them. Derek had become quite a loner. He seemed happy enough on the surface but his struggle with the losses he endured was overwhelming. He found it difficult to move on and no one judged him for that. He spent lots of time working and tending to the needs of all of us and never complained, but everyone knew he had inner turmoils that may not be fixed on this side of life.

I helped the children with the animal feeding to pass the time as we waited for the guys to return. They had followed the trail to the woods beyond Bob's property and there were places where the man sat down and rested and tried to stop his bleeding. He left behind his black balaclava and the wrapper of a feminine product. He was definitely still considered a threat. They tracked him to the highway nearly five miles away and lost all sign of his existence. He was likely picked up by a getaway vehicle along with the other two accomplices, but it was doubtful they would return after such a debacle. It seems they may have learned from the FGIA.

When they returned, we spent the next few days in preparation for our trip. The atmosphere surrounding us was positive. This was what we had wanted and although leaving Bob and Maggie was sad, we vowed to stay in touch. We left in our usual formation with Matt and Laura in front, in the Jeep, as we followed in the Chevy with the topper loaded with much of our gear. Eric and Rochelle brought up the rear in the multicolored Durango. We left Nebraska knowing that we would travel across the entire state of Wyoming, using campgrounds as our rest areas and one suggested home along the way to fuel up and re-supply. Supplies, however, were low, and once we had to rely on siphoning from old beat-up vehicles in a scrap metal junk yard. Some of the areas were so depleted of supplies and fuel that we waited over a week for gasoline, only to wait in long lines to get a rationed portion. We hunted, gathered, and filtered our water. We met some fine people at a roadside vegetable stand and were able to trade with them. This had become such a way of life for us, and we were so accustomed to hardships we rarely thought about the trivial pleasures life in Babylon afforded us. We were living a real life in pursuit of freedom that had also given us a satisfaction most people only dream of.

The home we had been instructed to visit along our route was abandoned. We pulled reluctantly into an overgrown drive that a cattle gate once protected, but the hinges were broken off. The door on the old white house was ajar and several windows were busted out. The entire place gave an eerie vibe, as though life came to an abrupt halt. There were junk cars in a row near the garage and a motor hanging from an A frame. Tools were scattered about on the floor as if someone might step out at any moment to continue their work. Matt and Eric called into the house but no answer came. A closer look revealed bullet holes all around the doors and windows, and inside were shell casings from 762's and .556's. There were blood stains on the floor and the steps of the porch. Inside it looked like couches and chairs were turned over to provide cover but to no avail. Blood was all through the house and the general consensus among us was that these people, who we were supposed to get help from, had been in a gun battle, which they had apparently lost. All things considered; we could not escape the haunting feeling that left us in agreement that we were not staying long. We secured the perimeter and scavenged the place for anything that would prosper our journey. There were gas cans full of gas, along with as many tools as we felt we could tolerate packing and fitting into our vehicles. There was no electricity in the home and the meter had been pulled. We didn't bother to even open the refrigerator, and the pantry was bare with the exception of a few canned vegetables, which we were inclined to leave.

The farther west we traveled the less populated the world became. If a person was able to stay away from cities and towns, one might pretend that the world was healing itself. In the attempt to create a White ethnostate there had been the generous combining of property from ranchers who collaborated in an effort to bring Whites into the area in numbers sustainable for growth. The farther into Idaho we went, the landscape varied between rugged mountain ranges and grassland valleys. The vastness alone made me feel small and even my large tract at Silver Springs dwarfed in comparison to what was available here. The people there were definitely like us, but the overall feeling was more subdued... not like Fern Grove. It seemed as though the consensus there was to live peacefully. Men were armed but the talk consisted mostly of growth in terms of houses, schools, medicine, churches, etc. One thing was agreed upon, no one other than White families were allowed to settle anywhere around us. That was when the gloves came off and these peaceable people became adamant and ready for violence against any non-White encroachment. Like Fern Grove, they had placed the right people in the positions necessary to promote White growth and deter any outsiders from coming in.

We were given a parcel of land to improve. As long as we were productive members of society, the land was never in question. It bordered a rugged National Park that the locals had taken from Federal Agents a few years prior. It now belonged to the people of Idaho who implemented their own hunting laws which I was happy to abide by. Through this implementation, I was able to feed our family with game and grow a garden. It was the simple life I had always wanted.

Land was deeded and recorded through the new government started by Elijah and Jackson who had escaped to Idaho prior to the fall of Fern Grove. Elijah was buried near the new courthouse and a large monument covered his tomb. In the same courthouse yard, there was a new national monument for a man named Ronald Weavley and Vivian, his wife. He and his family were early martyrs in the struggle to produce a free White ethnostate and their memories lingered as a rallying cry for those who continued in that same struggle.

Jackson had lost his wife and children during the siege at Fern Grove and never fully recovered mentally. He had taken his own life shortly after he received word that they had been brutally murdered.

We undertook building projects immediately. Our cabin was

constructed of logs and was barely under roof before Jessica gave birth to our daughter Eva. Once it was finished, we began work on a school that would double as a Church and Meeting house. We began to build a close-knit society with our core group, and it branched out as local people began to appreciate our ingenuity and desire for strength and stability. I was asked to teach theology at the Church twice a week and it seemed to come naturally. Matt and Eric were pillars with me in our community and we grew again in mind, faith and in spirit. Our homes were spread apart, and we would sometimes take day hikes to meet in the mountains so our children could play, and we could discuss our new lives.

One thing similar to Fern Grove was that not unlike the Oath we swore before, we signed our allegiance to the New Republic of Idaho. This meant that if Idaho went to war, I went to war. I honestly hoped it didn't come to that but if so, I knew it was the least I could do. I was pretty sure Matt and Eric felt the same.

When Eva was nearing her third birthday, Jessica became pregnant again. It became the most trying time we would have in Idaho. We did not have to fear the attacks from the third world here, but when the rogue American arm of the Jew order, which has been known for years as ZOG, engaged in a confrontation with the peoples of the newly declared republics, we had to defend ourselves. In my opinion, at least it was a nation of Whites in the biblical sense of the word, and I deemed it worth fighting for.

A group of hunters in an ex-national park, some one-hundred miles north of our homes, had been detained and one of them killed in a stand-off with a global military outfit. Evidently the area was still in dispute as a portion of the park existed in an area outside of the republic, although the Babylonian government did not recognize any of the holdings of the NROI. Matt, Eric, and I were called to the new state capital in Austraville. Due to our lack of formal military training, we sort of 'mustered-in' as privates although no one there viewed us as such. We deployed quickly, under the orders of Col. Hugh Wathen, a defector from the U.S. back in the teens. He had come to Idaho in search of a White homeland and was instrumental in capturing the parks from the ZOG. He was being called again to protect them.

I was elated to see the morale and confidence of the military-aged men within our ranks. We made no small showing as we approached the enemy force who was using our parks as a military staging area for their equipment. Firsthand knowledge of the situation proved to be a clear violation of trespass by the enemy with complete disregard and disrespect for the NROI.

Because of my well-known past, I was positioned as a sniper, which I felt comfortable doing from a vantage point given me through intelligence. I was better equipped than ever and felt safer than ever. Unfortunately, I was not able to be near Matthew and Eric which made me somewhat uneasy because we had been together for so long, and I felt a sense of responsibility for their safety. They were as good as family. Military engagements had devolved back into an age not dominated by technology. There were ground men of a foreign entity occupying our homeland and we wanted them physically removed. If they decided not to go after being told to leave, we would physically remove them. I had never been happier to hear a united force of White men stand on those principles and actually protect something greater than themselves. I knew it was a turning point. I was nearing fifty years old and had never once seen resolve in our race as I witnessed on this day.

I surveyed through my yardage scope all possible targets. I was able, from my location, to take out pilots trying to enter armed choppers so that any aerial attack would have been shut down immediately. I watched the men at the landing area and wondered how they could not understand what they were doing. I knew that through brainwashing, even when presented with truth, many will deny even when the truth is obvious. This mixture of foreign men and Aryan men alike seemed indifferent to their roll in trying to genocide the most giving, caring, empathetic race that ever existed on earth, and that was precisely why we had been reduced to an ethnostate in the far wilderness of the former U.S. instead of controlling and dominating the world over. At one time, as Moses predicted, our vine would stretch over the wall, and we would be hated for it.

I began to see activity among the helicopters. Checks were being performed on missiles, and they were putting fuel in some as they were starting others. Our communications had not specified if they were conducting training, retreating, or preparing to catch our forces off-guard with a missile assault. I had my radio man call and try to get clarification as I watched the pilots approach a couple of the choppers. I was running out of time if I was going to prevent an attack, but I could not be sure of the enemies' intentions. I didn't want to engage without permission even though in my heart I was ready to instigate a full-scale war. I was tired of these games. It seemed all we ever did was piddle around and just get smacked back to the ground. Enough of that. Word came just in time.

"Fire at will, Brother," my radio man said calmly and confidently.

It was all I needed. I waited until the first chopper barely lifted and I placed my bullet right between his aviator sunglasses. His dead weight pushed against his controls and sent the helicopter reeling out of control and made a huge mess as it crashed and burst

113

into flames several yards from its launch area. Quite the scenario unfolded. I was relentless, I took out three more pilots and several ground men before our location was detected. We took small arms fire for only a few seconds before we were out of sight. We were successful and the troops on the ground were overwhelming the enemy forces who were expecting air support but did not receive it. We scurried down a steep hillside, but my body was not what it used to be. I tried to stay in shape through those years, but I had to be nearing the end of my usefulness in the field. By the time we got to the HUM-V, my legs were shaking and going numb. The driver was getting the story from my radio man, and they were laughing and cheering as I sat in a state of satisfaction. I had done this before, there was no need to get overexcited. We circled around and came to the rear of the fighting, but I was unable to get out of the vehicle. I looked down at my lower extremities and saw that I was sitting in blood. The men with me helped me out of the vehicle and I had some sensations in my legs but not enough to hold myself up. I began to feel sick to my stomach as they laid me down on the ground at the base camp. I barely remembered seeing Col. Wathen just before the lights went out.

I saw Tiffany. She was dressed in white, and she was standing with my mother, also in white. A great light shined from behind them as Jessica and Lia appeared in front of them fully clothed in pale blue. It was as though they had asked permission to keep me. I may have stayed in that light with them for a thousand years or only a few moments, but however long it was, I knew my life was in question. I came to my senses long enough to hear a man say loudly, "Get her here as fast as you can... we have NO time."

Then I faded again. This time into a world unknown to me. I saw a small house on a stone foundation. In front stood a man similar in looks to my grandfather but it was not he. A woman came and took his hand and looked into my eyes as if she looked right through me. Their faces were vivid and clearer than real life. Again, Jessica stepped between them and me as if in petition against their beckoning.

I awoke again briefly and the men and women who moved about me seemed to be in a frantic state of slow motion. I left again. This time I saw my grandfather as a young man standing in front of the same old house only this time, I recognized it as my grandfather's homeplace, and a young boy stood beside him. I knew this was my father. He died young before I could know him. Again, Jessica and Lia appeared to talk with them. It looked as though they made a final desperate plea. The boy waived and I came to my senses through hearing the voices of the medical personnel. I saw Lia with a needle in her arm and a red tube extending from it. She was praying with tear-stained cheeks. Jessica was face down at my bedside with hands folded.

After I became stable enough to move, they airlifted me to a hospital in Austraville where we stayed for a few weeks until I could go home. Matt and Eric returned after their service was over. The victory that day had been complete and final. There would have been no reason for ZOG to desire that kind of ass whipping again. I was again decorated for service although I had never desired to be in the military as a young man, but I guess I was forced to wear the shoe that fit.

Life continued.

Word came again to us from Babylon that an infiltration of the old American military had taken place. Before Fern Grove fell, the armed forces in America had become just another arm of Jewish occupation and what they called the "Greater Israel Project." Under the direction of defectors who worked their way to top positions through deceiving their superiors, a group consisting of fighter pilots, naval men, and intelligence gatherers dealt the city of Tel Aviv a death blow. The land of Israel was reduced to a wasteland, and before the week was over, New York and Washington D.C. were reduced to rubble. Although the men who conducted these raids knew they would likely not live to sit under the tree they planted, and were ultimately killed, they inspired hundreds of thousands of White men to take action. War was hot in the east and as much as I wanted to join the efforts, I felt as though what was happening was a result of the work and life we, and others like us, had already lived.

By the time our next daughter was born I had turned forty-eight. Jessica and I had endured enough hardship and raising our families for the future was just as important as fighting to protect them. When the discussion came up between Eric, Matt, and me about the possibility of joining some sort of National military arm, we agreed to grow old this time. Matt was even older than I.

I continued to teach the glory of God and the coming kingdom on earth, 'wherein dwelleth righteousness.' I hunted game in the mountains and worshipped God in everything I did. Jessica sang with all her might in the church and moved people to tears of joy with her angelic voice. People began to flock to hear the Word of God and learn about their heritage and their special place in the will of God.

I watched the relationship between Lia and Jeremiah grow and when the time came, Jessica sewed the dress she would wear the day we celebrated their marriage. They were young but mature enough, and nothing prevented them from starting their own family. It was a joyous occasion. Marrying and bringing souls into the world had become popular among our people again, and large families blossomed as I married many couples at our little Church.

I will never forget the trip to the lake the summer after Lia was married. Our children played at a distance on the sand bar and swam, the older children playing with the younger children as they laughed and frolicked in joyful games.

She lay beside me on the blanket we had stretched out on the sand. She took off the thin cotton robe she was wearing over her bathing suit. Time and babies had taken their toll on Jessica's body, but I could not be unattracted to her. She was elegant and still pretty, with that war eagle above her breast. As she lay her head on my chest I remember wishing for this moment long, long ago...